PRAISE FOR TAMMY L. GRACE

"*A Season of Hope* is a perfect holiday read! Warm wonderful and gentle tale reflecting small town romance at its best."
— *Jeanie, review of A Season for Hope: A Christmas Novella*

"This book is a clean, simple romance with a background story very similar to the works of Debbie Macomber. If you like Macomber's books you will like this one. The main character, Hope and her son Jake are on a road trip when their car breaks down, thus starts the story. A holiday tale filled with dogs, holiday fun, and the joy of giving will warm your heart.
— *Avid Mystery Reader, review of A Season for Hope: A Christmas Novella*

"This book was just as enchanting as the others. Hardships with the love of a special group of friends. I recommend the series as a must read. I loved every exciting moment. A new author for me. She's fabulous."
—*Maggie!, review of Pieces of Home: A Hometown Harbor Novel (Book 4)*

"Tammy is an amazing author, she reminds me of Debbie Macomber… Delightful, heartwarming…just down to earth."

— *Plee, review of A Promise of Home: A Hometown Harbor Novel (Book 3)*

"This was an entertaining and relaxing novel. Tammy Grace has a simple yet compelling way of drawing the reader into the lives of her characters. It was a pleasure to read a story that didn't rely on theatrical tricks, unrealistic events or steamy sex scenes to fill up the pages. Her characters and plot were strong enough to hold the reader's interest."

—*MrsQ125, review of Finding Home: A Hometown Harbor Novel (Book 1)*

"This is a beautifully written story of loss, grief, forgiveness and healing. I believe anyone could relate to the situations and feelings represented here. This is a read that will stay with you long after you've completed the book."

—*Cassidy Hop, review of Finally Home: A Hometown Harbor Novel (Book 5)*

Killer Music and Deadly Connection are award-winning novels, earning the 2016 & 2017 Mystery Gold Medal by the Global E-Book Awards

"Killer Music is a clever and well-crafted whodunit. The vivid and colorful characters shine as the author gradually reveals their hidden secrets—an absorbing page-turning read."

— *Jason Deas, bestselling author of Pushed and Birdsongs*

"I could not put this book down! It was so well written & a suspenseful read! This is definitely a 5-star story! I'm hoping there will be a sequel!"

—*Colleen, review of Killer Music*

"This is the best book yet by this author. The plot was well crafted with an unanticipated ending. I like to try to leap ahead and see if I can accurately guess the outcome. I was

able to predict some of the plot but not the actual details which made reading the last several chapters quite engrossing."
—*0001PW, review of Deadly Connection*

THE MAGIC OF THE SEASON

CHRISTMAS IN SILVER FALLS

TAMMY L. GRACE

LONE MOUNTAIN PRESS

The Magic of the Season
A Christmas novella by
Tammy L. Grace

The Magic of the Season is a work of fiction. Names, characters, places, and incidents either are products of the author's imagination or are used fictitiously. Any resemblance to actual events, locales, entities, or persons, living or dead, is entirely coincidental.

THE MAGIC OF THE SEASON Copyright © 2019 by Tammy L. Grace

All rights reserved. No part of this book may be reproduced or transmitted in any form or by any means, electronic or mechanical including photocopying, recording, or by any information storage and retrieval system without the written permission of the author, except for the use of brief quotations in a book review. For permissions contact the author directly via electronic mail: tammy@tammylgrace.com

www.tammylgrace.com
Facebook: https://www.facebook.com/tammylgrace.books
Twitter: @TammyLGrace
Instagram: @authortammylgrace

Published in the United States by Lone Mountain Press, Nevada

ISBN 978-1-945591-11-2 (eBook)
ISBN 978-1-945591-21-1 (paperback)
FIRST EDITION
Printed in the United States of America

ALSO BY TAMMY L. GRACE

HOMETOWN HARBOR SERIES
Hometown Harbor: The Beginning FREE prequel

Finding Home

Home Blooms

A Promise of Home

Pieces of Home

Finally Home

Forever Home

Hometown Harbor Series Books 1-3

COOPER HARRINGTON DETECTIVE SERIES
Killer Music

Deadly Connection

Dead Wrong

Cooper Harrington Detective Novels Books 1-3

CHRISTMAS STORIES
A Season for Hope (Christmas in Silver Falls Book 1)

The Magic of the Season (Christmas in Silver Falls Book 2)

Christmas in Snow Valley

Christmas Sisters (Soul Sisters at Cedar Mountain Lodge Book 1)

Christmas Wishes (Soul Sisters at Cedar Mountain Lodge Book 3)

GLASS BEACH COTTAGE SERIES
Beach Haven

WRITING AS CASEY WILSON
A Dog's Hope

A Dog's Chance

Tammy would love to connect with readers on social media and her website at www.tammylgrace.com. Remember to subscribe to her mailing list and you'll receive the fun interview she did with the dogs from her Hometown Harbor Series as an exclusive free gift only available to her subscribers. **Subscribe here: https://wp.me/P9umIy-e**

Follow Tammy on Facebook and click over and follow Tammy on BookBub and Amazon by clicking the follow buttons on her pages.

Wishing you and yours a bit of magic this season

THE MAGIC OF THE SEASON
CHRISTMAS IN SILVER FALLS

Book 2

1

Madison stepped up to the counter of her favorite juicery and touched her credit card to the machine at the register. "Have a nice day, Ms. White," said the young woman who handed Madison a tall cup of her standing order. A green power smoothie.

"Same to you," said Madison as she adjusted her sunglasses and walked the two blocks to the modern glass building where she spent her days at Conwell Advertising and Marketing. The palm trees lining the walkway rustled in the ocean breeze. It was Friday, and the weekend promised even more sunshine.

She nodded to the security guard at the desk downstairs and took the elevator to the top floor. Her assistant, Paige, greeted her and followed Madison down the hallway to her corner office with a view of the ocean in Manhattan Beach. "Mr. Conwell wants to see you as soon as you get settled," said Paige.

Madison nodded and tucked her purse into a drawer. "I'll be right there."

She checked her calendar while she sipped her drink. The

intercom buzzed, and Paige announced, "Your mom is on the line for you."

Madison hit the button and said, "Hey, Mom, I'm on my way into a meeting. What's up?"

"Nothing new. Working on some orders for a big delivery tomorrow over in Crystal Valley. Trying to get organized for the festival. I have more orders than I know how to handle. How are you doing, sweetie?"

"Fine, just busy. I have all the confirmations for our vacation. We leave on January second. Your flight from Reno down here is all set. Paige should have emailed you the ticket information. I'll meet you at the airport. Hawaii sounds heavenly right now."

"I can't wait. It will be wonderful to see you. Being in Hawaii is a bonus."

"It will be terrific," said Madison, eyeing the notes on her desk. "I'll call you this weekend when I have more time. I need to run, Mom."

"Okay, I'll talk to you later. Love you lots."

Madison disconnected and grabbed a notepad before hurrying down the hall.

With great care, Grant guided his bakery delivery van around the sharp turn on the icy road outside of Silver Falls early Saturday morning. The sun had risen but was obscured by the heavy cloud cover, making the trip even more treacherous.

Few cars were on the slick roads, as he trekked along to deliver a large pastry order to a neighboring town. As he slowed for another turn, the reflection of headlights shining against the trees on the side of the road caught his eye. He flicked on his hazard lights and pulled to a spot on the road with a wide shoulder.

He shivered as he climbed from the van to investigate. As he neared the source of the lights, he hurried. He recognized the vehicle with its signature red and green Sugar Shop logo. "Peggy," he yelled. "It's Grant. I'm coming."

He pulled out his cell phone and shut his eyes in a silent prayer, hoping he was in a spot with service. The signal was weak, but he stabbed the numbers. He reached an emergency dispatcher and reported the accident, repeating his location numerous times as the connection deteriorated and the voice of the dispatcher became choppy.

Peggy's van was angled in a ravine alongside the road. It looked like she had skidded off the side and went over the embankment. Grant surveyed the area and started his climb down the steep terrain.

He took it slow, thankful for the hiking boots he had worn. He slid a bit but caught himself on the van as he glided into it. When he reached the driver's window, he sucked in a breath. Peggy's head was bleeding, and her eyes were closed.

It took some prying, but he wrenched open the door. "Peggy, Peggy," he put a gentle hand on her shoulder. "Can you hear me?"

She moaned but didn't respond. "Come on, Peggy, open your eyes."

He took in the crumpled hood of the van and looked down at Peggy's legs. The blood on her jeans and the unnatural position of her right leg made him wince. He reached across the seat, grabbed Peggy's heavy jacket, and tucked it around her.

He took off his glove and put his fingers against her neck. Finding her pulse, he breathed a sigh of relief. He knew the danger in trying to move her and elected to hold her hand instead. "Hurry, hurry, please," he whispered.

The blood dripping from Peggy's head prompted him to unzip his jacket and use his pocket knife to cut off the bottom of the t-shirt he wore under his heavy flannel one. He used it as a makeshift compress and applied it to the cut on Peggy's head. She flinched and gasped. "I'm sorry, Peggy. I just want to slow this bleeding."

After several more minutes, he heard the faint sound of sirens in the distance. "They're almost here. Just a few more minutes, Peggy." He squeezed her hand to reassure her. She moaned again.

The flashing blue and red lights from all the vehicles converging on the road above bounced off the snow-covered trees. Loud voices, doors slamming, and the rush of footsteps followed. "Down here. She's down here. We need medical help," Grant yelled.

The firefighters and paramedics, all of whom Grant knew by name, eased him out of the way and went about their work, checking Peggy and freeing her from the vehicle. Grant made his way up to the road. A deputy put a blanket around him and led him to one of the units, parked and running with its lights flashing.

"Hey, Todd," Grant nodded his appreciation.

The deputy made sure the heater was turned on high and promised to return in a few minutes.

Grant watched the activity as the group of volunteer firemen emerged from the side of the road carrying a stretcher. They loaded Peggy into the ambulance, and it rushed down the road.

Todd returned and asked Grant several questions for his report. After Todd closed his notebook, Grant sighed and asked, "Do you think I could go down and get Peggy's deliveries out of the back of her van? I know she'll be worried about her candy."

The deputy nodded. "The paramedics got her talking a

little when they loaded her, and she was worried about the deliveries. I told her we'd take care of it. I know Peggy would appreciate you doing that. We're going to have to tow it. We can help you get the stuff out of the back."

Grant nodded. "I'll put it in my van and take care of it. I'm sure she was doing her weekly run to Crystal Valley. I'm heading there with my delivery. It's not a problem."

While Todd organized the emptying of the Sugar Shop's deliveries from the back of the van, Grant called his customer and explained he was running a bit behind due to an accident. With the help of the deputies, it didn't take long to load the tins of Peggy's famous fudge and caramels. Grant found her delivery clipboard and paperwork and added it to his front seat.

Grant thanked them and waved goodbye as he steered back onto the road. After his delivery, he made stops at the three stores Peggy supplied and explained she had been in an accident.

Everyone loved Peggy. Her longtime customers expressed their concern and dismay at the news. When it became apparent that he wouldn't be leaving anytime soon, Grant called his bakery back in Silver Falls to let them know he would be delayed.

Word spread quickly, and the townsfolk gathered at the last stop, a small café that sold Peggy's fudge and caramels during the holidays. The owner treated Grant to lunch while everyone gathered to talk about Peggy.

Grant promised to let them know as soon as he received word on her condition. He left with lots of hugs and well wishes, plus a huge cup of coffee for the trip home.

After an uneventful journey back to Silver Falls, Grant finished his day at the bakery, picked up Luna and Ginger from home, and drove to his mom's for dinner. He saw Drew's SUV in the driveway when he pulled behind the Silver Falls Guest House. As he admired the decorations and lights he and Drew had helped his mom install this past weekend, he smiled. Thanksgiving was only a few days away, but his mom was ready for Christmas.

Last year she had taken a nasty fall while decorating. This year the two brothers were taking no chances. She wasn't allowed to use a ladder or carry anything up and down the stairs. He ushered the dogs through the back door and was greeted with the delicious smell of dinner.

"There you are, Grant. Any news on Peggy?" asked Dottie, as she added a generous pat of butter to a mountain of mashed potatoes.

"Todd stopped by the bakery and said they were transporting her to Reno. She needs surgery on her leg. Sounds like that's the worst of it. She also injured the knee on her other leg, her wrist is sprained, and she's got a deep cut on her head."

Dottie shook her head as she added the biscuits to the table. "Drew," she hollered, "Dinner's ready. You guys come on."

Drew came around the corner, his arm around Hope, with Jake trailing behind, followed by their two dogs. Last year over the holidays, Hope and her son had been unexpected guests at Dottie's. After losing his wife and son years ago, Drew had fallen in love with Hope and her son in the weeks she spent in Silver Falls. The two had married in the summer. Hope helped Dottie with the guest house and RV park during the busy seasons, volunteered at Jake's school, and made Drew the happiest veterinarian in town.

"I'd like to go visit Peggy tomorrow. Do you think you

could take some time off and we could drive over to check on her?" Dottie raised her brows at Grant.

He nodded as he bit into a warm biscuit. "Yeah, I think that's a good idea. We can find out if she needs anything."

"She's going to be out of commission at her busiest time of year," said Dottie.

"Her famous fudge she used to make for her friends has grown into quite the successful business," said Drew.

"She was sort of forced into it when Eddie died so long ago. She had to support her daughter, and she's worked hard to turn it into a thriving business. Despite her addition of the ice cream parlor in the summer, I know she makes the bulk of her money over the Christmas season." Dottie passed a platter to Hope.

"We can find out if she needs anything done around the house while she's in the hospital," suggested Grant.

"It's heartbreaking. I'm not sure how she'll make it without her holiday sales. There's no way she can work with all those injuries." Tears filled Dottie's eyes. "It will be months." She reached for a tissue. "She volunteered to coordinate the fundraiser this year too."

"We'll do all we can to help her. We'll start with a visit tomorrow and find out what she needs. I know the whole community loves Peggy and would do everything possible to help her." Grant gave his mother a reassuring look.

Hope squeezed Dottie's hand. "Trust me. I know what the people of Silver Falls are capable of, especially at Christmas. I couldn't have imagined my situation last year." She gazed across the table at Drew. "Who would have guessed that my broken-down car would lead me to love and happiness I never dreamed were possible?"

2

After getting the bulk of his work done at the bakery, Grant took off at noon. Dottie left Hope in charge of the guest house and let Grant drive her car down the mountain to Reno. He dropped her off in front of the hospital and promised to meet up with her in Peggy's room.

He slipped the car into a spot in the parking garage and navigated the maze of pathways and banks of elevators. Peggy's room was on the seventh floor. Grant checked the signage and started down the hall.

He passed by a sitting area and turned his head to check the room numbers. As he glanced away, a woman, holding a cup of coffee and talking on her cell phone, ran into him, splashing the warm liquid all over both of them.

She gasped and said, "I've got to call you back." She looked down at her shirt. "Great. Terrific. Just what I need."

Grant brushed at the splotches of coffee on his jacket. "No real harm, I guess." He shrugged.

She let out a heavy sigh. "No harm? This is a silk blouse." She directed her merciless glare at Grant.

He took in her shiny hair with sunkissed highlights and a

casual style that looked carefree but sophisticated. He looked into her dagger-like eyes, deep blue like a stormy sea. The only recognizable feature of the skinny, plain girl he remembered from high school was her eyes. They changed depending on her mood. They could be tropical blue, steely blue, or dark and foreboding like today. Despite their mothers' friendship during their childhood and all the time they spent together, their relationship had changed when she was in high school. "Sugar, is that you?"

Her stunning eyes widened, and a crease formed between her brows. "Nobody calls me Sugar. It's Madison." There was a definite snap in her reply. She stared at him for another moment and said, "Grant?" The hard stare softened. "I didn't recognize you. Mom told me you're the one who helped her." She shrugged and gave him a sheepish look. "Sorry about the coffee."

He held up his hands and smiled. "No problem. I never wear silk."

She grimaced when she looked at the brown blotches covering her white blouse. "I've got my suitcase in the rental car with some spare clothes. I'd forgotten how cold it gets here though. I'm going to have to go shopping for some warmer clothes and a coat."

"And some gloves and boots would be a good idea. We've got snow already." He offered to get her another cup of coffee and returned a few minutes later. She was on her phone when he placed the cup on the table next to her chair.

He sipped on his coffee and watched Sugar as she discussed a work project. The ordinary brown-haired girl from his childhood, who had played at his house and swam in the lake when they were growing up, was unrecognizable. The stylish and attractive woman who sat before him, wearing designer skinny jeans, suede ankle boots with heels, and a fancy blouse, did not gel with his memories.

After her dad died, Sugar had changed. The carefree tomboy, always up for anything, had withdrawn. She spent most of her time alone, holed up in her room, drawing and sketching. In high school, she was a loner. Artsy and detached. She was two years behind Grant, and they hadn't had any classes together. She ended up getting a scholarship to an art and design school in New York, left for college, and never came back to Silver Falls.

She disconnected and took a long sip from her cup. "Thanks, I appreciate it."

"What's it been, about twenty years since I've seen you? I guess last time you were in Silver Falls was when you left for college, right?"

She nodded. "I know I should have come home more. Back then, I couldn't wait to leave. I guess I never looked back."

"And I never left." He shrugged and grinned.

"My job is crazy. It's been easier over the years to have Mom visit me. We've had a tradition of taking a trip together right after Christmas, when her business is slow and I can take some time off from work. Sometimes she just stays with me, but we've gone on several cruises and tropical vacations. It's nice to spend time in warmer weather in the winter. We were supposed to leave for Hawaii right after the first of the year."

"I know Peggy always looks forward to the time she spends with you. So, you're still in Los Angeles?" he asked.

She nodded. "I live in Santa Monica and work in Manhattan Beach. They're both considered to be part of the Los Angeles area."

"No wonder you're cold. You're a beach bum now." Grant chuckled.

She looked across and stared at the window showcasing

the snow-capped mountains. "It's definitely easy to adjust to life there."

"How's your mom doing today?" Grant took another drink from his cup.

"It's going to be a long road to recovery. They did surgery yesterday on her leg. She's going to have to go to a rehab place. She can't do much for herself until her wrist heals. The doctor wants her doing physical therapy, and she'll get that there. It's going to take months for her leg to heal. She's not too excited about the idea."

"I don't blame her. I'm sure she's worried about the shop."

"That's an understatement. She wants me to stay and take care of her orders. You know how protective she is of her fudge recipe. Nobody knows it." She rolled her eyes.

"She has good reason. It's the best in the world." He drummed his fingers on the arm of the chair. "Are you going to be able to stay in Silver Falls?"

She blew out a breath that fluttered her bangs. "I don't know. My job is so busy this time of year. I'm not sure how I can make it all work. I'm really not cut out for candy making."

Grant asked about her work, and she explained she worked for a major advertising firm and was the assistant creative director. "We've got a few important projects to wrap up before the end of the year."

"I know your mom makes the majority of her income this time of year. I'm sure it's weighing on her, Sugar."

She smiled. "I guess I'm not going to be able to shake my nickname here, huh?"

Grant shrugged and grinned. "Sorry. I've just always known you as Sugar. So has everyone else in Silver Falls. They will be so excited to see you. We talked about her situation last night, and we'll do all we can to help Peggy…and you."

She nodded. "That's kind of you. I need to figure it out. They're going to transfer her in a couple of days. I've got to talk to my boss."

"Does she need anything done at the house?"

Her eyes widened. "I'm going to head there tonight. Try to figure out what to do with her candy orders and find a solution."

"You can follow us back to Silver Falls if you want," he offered as he stood.

"I might do that, thanks."

"I better go find Mom and check on Peggy. We can hang out here as long as you want to stay," said Grant.

"I've got a few more calls to make, and then I'll come to her room." She pointed down the hallway.

Grant left her to her cell phone and found his mom and Peggy jabbering and laughing. "Oh, there he is. My knight in shining armor." Peggy lifted her hands, with her wrists in braces. "Come here, you sweet boy."

They spent the next hour listening to Peggy's nonstop praise of Grant. He passed along all the well wishes from Crystal Valley. Flowers arrived while they chatted, and Dottie took care in arranging them around the room and reading Peggy each message.

The mayor, firemen, deputies, and her book club had sent Peggy huge bouquets, as had many of the business owners from downtown. Tears dotted Peggy's cheeks as she listened to the heartfelt words and gazed at the arrangements.

"I ran into Sugar in the hallway." Grant chuckled. "Literally. We had a coffee accident. She said she'll follow us back to Silver Springs tonight. I told her we'll all help out and get things taken care of for you. So don't you worry about anything. Your only jobs now are to heal, rest, and do your therapy."

The Magic of the Season

"She likes to be called Madison, you know?" Peggy whispered through her tears.

"She did mention that." Grant winked and added, "I told her it probably wasn't gonna happen. Silver Falls knows her as Sugar."

Peggy sniffled. "There's just so much to do. All the candy orders, plus the arts fundraiser. I've barely started on that work. They're counting on the money raised to keep the programs going. Without it, they're going to have to discontinue them."

A nurse came through the door and said, "It's time for your meds."

"We'll be outside," said Dottie, bending to kiss her friend on the forehead, taking care to stay clear of the bandage that covered half of it.

Grant led his mom to the sitting area where they spotted Sugar talking on her phone. He bent down to get in her line of vision.

She hurried her conversation and ended the call. "Mrs. Fisher," she said, standing to greet them. "It's been so long."

Dottie embraced the young woman in a long hug. "It's Dottie to you, sweetie. It's wonderful to see you, Sugar."

"I was trying to get work situated so I could spend some time here and do my best to help Mom."

Dottie held Sugar's hands between hers. "I would hope your boss would understand such an emergency."

Sugar nodded. "He does. However, it's a critical time at the firm for several projects."

"We'll do whatever we can to help," said Dottie.

"We should try to head back before it gets dark. With the low temperatures, the roads can be icy," said Grant.

"That works for me. I haven't driven on ice in ages. The last thing we need is another accident." Sugar gathered her purse and headed back down the hallway.

Less than an hour later, she emerged, and Grant and Dottie poked their heads in Peggy's doorway to wish her a good night. The three of them made their way out of the hospital and to the parking garage.

"We'll wait for you at the exit," said Grant. He described Dottie's car, and Sugar said she was driving a red SUV.

"I do need to stop and get some warmer clothes. I'd probably have more luck here than in Silver Falls. Is there a place to stop on our way?"

Grant nodded. "There's a giant outdoor store right off the highway. We can make a quick stop there."

A few minutes later, they were on their way. Grant and Dottie wandered the huge store while they waited for Sugar to pick out some clothes. After perusing the selection of goods, Dottie and Grant stationed themselves on a bench outside of the dressing room area.

Sugar went in and out of the dressing room, mumbling each time. "I only wear black and white. Occasionally gray. But not these plaids or bright colors." She rifled through racks and walked by, taking more clothes with her.

Grant surveyed his plaid flannel shirt and Dottie's bright red parka. He glanced at his mom and rolled his eyes. "Wow," he said in a quiet voice. "Does it really matter what color her clothes are?"

Dottie grinned. "She's very chic. I'm sure she's used to more options. She's been a city girl for a very long time. It's going to take her some time to remember what it's like in Silver Falls. Nobody cares what kind of clothes you wear. It's what's inside that counts."

After a longer stop than Grant had anticipated, and carrying more bags than he could imagine, they were on the road home. Sugar was outfitted in sturdy boots, a sweater, gloves, and a heavy winter jacket. All in black. Grant led the way to Dottie's house.

The Magic of the Season

After much cajoling, Sugar agreed to accept Dottie's invitation to dinner. Dottie called Hope as soon as they were on the road to alert her to their dinner guest. Dottie dozed on the hour ride back to Silver Falls but woke as soon as Grant made the turn off the main road.

As they navigated the steps to the house, Grant offered each of the women an arm and held the front door for them. The aroma of roasted chicken wafted from the house. Drew stood near the entry holding back the inquisitive pack of five dogs.

"Welcome, Sugar. I hope you don't mind dogs," said Drew, offering her a smile.

"Hi, Drew. Nice to see you. I don't have time for a dog, but I like them." Grant joined his brother and gave the dogs a few scratches and ear rubs while Dottie made her way to the kitchen.

Drew introduced the furry friends by name and let them go to greet Sugar. Scout, who was Dottie's loyal golden retriever, nuzzled Sugar with her nose. Fletch and Dickens, Drew's two goldens, inched closer for attention. Luna, a sleek black Labrador retriever, and another reddish copper colored golden named Ginger, greeted Grant with enthusiastic tail wags, having missed their master.

After all five dogs had inspected Sugar with their inquisitive noses and received a few pets on the head, they moved into the living room and sat in front of the fire.

"Come on in," Drew waved. I'll introduce you to my wife. She's in charge of dinner tonight.

Sugar gazed around the house as she followed Drew. "This place is just how I remembered. It looks so festive with all the Christmas decorations. I don't even bother to put up a tree."

Dottie thanked her and said, "I've got to get them up early, or it gets too busy around here. We've got a full house starting Wednesday, then Thanksgiving, and then the festival. It's nonstop until the new year."

Drew took Hope's hand and urged her from behind the island counter. "This is Hope, my wife. We got married this past summer."

"Lovely to meet you, Sugar," said Hope. "I'm so sorry about your mother. I've treated my son to many ice cream cones at her shop."

Drew left them to chat while he finished getting the serving platters on the table. "Jake," he yelled out. "Dinner's ready."

The clomp of feet rushing down the hall from Dottie's wing of the house announced his arrival. Hope introduced him to Sugar. "Nice to meet you," said Jake, offering her a handshake.

Drew explained that Sugar was the daughter of the woman who owned the Sugar Shop, one of Jake's favorite treat spots. "I've never met anyone named Sugar. That's so cool," said the boy, admiring their guest.

"My real name is Madison. My dad always called me Sugar when I was little, and it stuck. Then Mom used it in her business name." She smirked and added, "This is Silver Falls though, and nothing changes here."

Hope slipped her arm around Drew's waist. "I'm thankful it doesn't change. It's a wonderful town, full of kind and genuine people. Jake and I broke down here last year around this time and fell in love." Hope glanced at her husband. "I've never experienced anything like it."

Grant stole a warm roll from the basket and said, "Come on guys, I'm starving." They gathered around the table, listening to Dottie reminisce about her younger days with Peggy and memories of raising their children. She told Sugar about her bad fall last year.

"That's how Hope came to stay with us," said Dottie with

a smile. "Without her and Jake," she winked at the boy, "I would have never made it through my busy season."

"Just like you said, Dottie, we ended up here for a reason." Tears filled Hope's eyes. "Now we're lucky enough to call Silver Falls home and all of you family."

3

The next morning after doing some work at the bakery, Grant stopped by Peggy's Victorian house at the end of Main Street. She had lived there as long as he could remember. The first floor had been converted into her store, with a sitting room and office in the back. She made her home in the upper two floors.

He found Sugar in the kitchen going through orders. He handed her a small pink box from the bakery. "Thought you might be hungry."

"Oh, that's nice of you. I try not to eat sugar. Or bread. I was hoping to get a green smoothie this morning. Where might I find one?"

"Uh," he stammered. "I have no idea. Your mom makes fruit smoothies, but only in the summer."

"They're at all the coffee shops where I live. You should add them to your menu at the bakery."

Grant's brows arched. "I've never had anyone ask for one, but I'll keep it in mind." He looked at the order sheets on the counter. "Are you getting a handle on everything here?"

"I'm not sure how Mom does this all by herself." She

pointed at the papers. "I remember the festival from when I was growing up here, but I never dreamed she would have this many orders."

"I know with the accident you don't have a delivery van. I'm happy to deliver your orders when I'm doing mine each day."

Her eyes widened in surprise. "Wow, that would be terrific. That would solve one problem."

"We get our supplies delivered once a week here. If you need to place an order, you need to do it by three o'clock tomorrow. Thanksgiving has the schedule messed up this week, so the truck will come on Tuesday."

"Oh, that's good to know. I hate to call Mom with a bunch of questions and have her worry about me handling things. I'll see if I can find her past invoices for this time of year and try to duplicate what she normally requests."

"Good idea. You'll probably need to increase quantities for this year. They added another event this year during the festival. There's a fundraiser for the Silver Falls Arts Center at the old schoolhouse. There was talk of it being a multi-day event. Your mom actually volunteered to coordinate it. It's the week before Christmas with a huge party on Christmas Eve."

"They're going to have to find someone else for that." Tears filled her eyes, and the pitch of her voice rose. "There's no way I can do one more thing."

Grant put his hand on her arm. "It's going to be okay. We'll figure it out."

She pulled her arm away from him and shook her head. "This is a disaster." She perused her mother's files and found the one related to the annual festival. "To say the festival has grown over the years would be an understatement." Her eyes widened as she read the recap of sales. "When I was a kid, I don't remember it being such a big deal."

"It seems like every few years we add new activities. We get more out-of-town visitors now. I think the merchant association started posting a few things online in an effort to entice tourists. I'm always slammed with the cookie exchange, not to mention all the other events. It can be overwhelming."

She flipped through the pages in the file and nodded. "I'm beginning to feel that way already."

"From what I know, your mom doesn't get that much walk-in traffic until the festival starts the weekend after Thanksgiving. You could probably keep the storefront closed this week and work on getting orders ready. Folks will understand. Just leave a note on the door and have them call and leave you a message if they need something."

She nodded in agreement. "Makes sense. Then I'll have to figure out what to do for the next four weeks of the festival."

"And, you'll have to get this place decorated for Christmas. Your mom always has this place looking like a gingerbread house during the holidays."

"She's got plastic tubs full of decorations and lights in the storeroom. I'm not sure I'm going to have time to worry about all that. It's more Mom's thing."

"How's she doing today? Have you talked to her?" asked Grant.

"They're getting her ready to be moved tomorrow. She's going to the rehabilitation center. She's convinced she'll be home by Christmas. I'm going to go visit once she's settled there and bring her a few things from home." Her cell phone rang. "At least it's working now. I wasn't getting a signal earlier." She let out a long sigh. "It's work. I'll talk to you later."

"Cell service can be spotty here." Grant gave her a wave and headed for his house. He retrieved his dogs and set out

The Magic of the Season

for his mother's house and Sunday dinner. He found Dottie and Hope in the kitchen.

Grant slid into a chair at the granite-topped island. He nicked a few bites of apple from the cutting board Dottie was using. She waved her knife at him. "That's a good way to lose a finger, young man."

"What have you been up to today?" asked Hope.

"Just a little work. Stopped by Peggy's place to check on Sugar." He slipped another piece of apple into his mouth. "She's trying to do her own work and handle Peggy's orders. I'm not sure she's up to it. Not to mention she doesn't even decorate for Christmas."

Drew and Jake trudged into the kitchen with the empty bowl of snacks they had enjoyed while watching football. "Who doesn't decorate for Christmas?" asked Drew.

Dottie looked up from her pie. "Grant was telling us he stopped and saw Sugar. She's a bit overwhelmed with all the tasks at hand."

Drew wiggled his brows. "Maybe we should help her. We could handle the decorating." He gave Dottie a grin. "After all, we had the best teacher."

She smiled at him. "That's a wonderful idea. Why don't you boys go over there and get that done this afternoon while the weather is nice? Bring Sugar back here for dinner when you're done."

Jake jumped up and down. "Yay, I love to decorate."

Grant's brow furrowed. "I don't know, Mom. Sugar isn't the same. She's sort of on edge. I told her about the fundraiser, and she almost had a meltdown. She thinks they'll have to find someone else to coordinate it."

"I'm happy to help with it," offered Hope. "I know how important the arts center is to the town."

Bundled up in coats and hats, Drew and Jake came into

the kitchen. "Let's get going so we can get this done before dark," said Drew.

Dottie held up a finger. "Just make sure you do Peggy proud. She's always been very particular about her decorations."

The two brothers and Jake set off in Drew's truck with ladders and a few supplies, promising to be home for dinner.

Drew and Jake went about setting up the ladders while Grant went inside to let Sugar know what they were doing. He found her on the same chair in the kitchen, finalizing her order for supplies, bundled in a scarf and coat, with a blanket around her. "Hey, Sugar. Are you okay?"

Her mouth was covered with the scarf, and she pulled it down to talk. "I'm freezing. I can't seem to get warm."

Grant shrugged. "It feels warm enough. Probably just not used to our weather. You could bump up the thermostat."

"I did that. It didn't seem to make much difference."

"Well, we had some spare time this afternoon and thought we'd come over and put up your outdoor decorations and lights."

"Really? That's nice of you. It's not at all necessary. I'm sure we could forgo one year."

"Mom said it's important to Peggy, and we know how finicky she is about the decorations. She likes it to look the same each year. We know how she does it. She usually gets one of the guys from the hardware store to hang them, and she supervises." He laughed and added, "Jake is super excited to help."

She shrugged. "If you guys want to do it, I won't stop you." She stood and led the way to the storeroom. "All the decorations are in here."

The Magic of the Season

He started gathering the plastic bins. "Mom said to bring you back for dinner tonight. She and Hope are cooking up a storm."

She shook her head. "Oh, I can eat something here. I need to run to the market anyway. I can grab something there. A salad or some soup." She mentioned a grocery chain that included a salad bar and prepared foods.

"You won't find one of those yuppified places here. We've only got the Silver Falls Market, and they close early on Sundays. All the restaurants are closed by noon."

She rolled her eyes. "I'm reminded of why I left this place. Don't they know how inconvenient that is? You would think they could have stepped into the current century by now. I don't know how you live here."

Grant bit his tongue and carried a stack of totes outside. He left Sugar rambling on to herself about all the reasons she was glad she didn't live in Silver Falls.

After sorting through the bins, he found the lights. He and Drew worked together to string them around the porch, roofline, and all the windows, with Jake supervising from the ground. Next, they wrapped the columns on the porch with wide red ribbon, making them look like candy canes. As the light faded from the sky, they tackled the bushes and trees, putting Jake in charge of all the work that didn't require ladders.

It was dark when they finished. Drew connected the timer and turned on the lights. "Wow, it looks so cool," yelled Jake. The two brothers joined Jake and stood on the front walkway. A huge grin filled the boy's face, and colorful lights reflected in his excited eyes.

"We do good work," said Drew. He snapped a photo with his phone. "We'll send this to Peggy, and it should make her smile."

Grant carried the empty bins back inside. He heard Sugar

on her cell phone. "Just email me the presentations, and we can set up a call to discuss them tomorrow. I'm going to have to stay here and take care of my mom's business while she's recuperating." With an exasperated sigh, she added, "I don't think I can stand it here for a whole month. I'll have to see how it goes."

He shut the storeroom door and walked into the kitchen as she disconnected the call. "We're going to head back to dinner. Mom will be disappointed if you don't come."

Grant heard the clomp of Jake's boots as he came through the door. "Let's go, Grant. Drew's waiting."

Sugar grabbed her purse and followed them outside. "Wow, I can't believe you guys did all this," she said, taking in the house from the sidewalk. "It looks wonderful. Just like when I was growing up here."

"Wait until you see the Festival of Lights. Maybe you'll get a spark of your Christmas spirit back," said Grant.

Jake grinned and pointed out the bushes he had decorated to Sugar. "Let's go big-guy," said Drew, hefting him into the truck.

"I'll follow you guys," said Sugar, shivering as she climbed behind the wheel of her rental.

Over a delicious meal and the promise of fresh apple pie, the Fisher clan regaled Sugar with their plans for the upcoming Festival of Lights. Jake's eyes sparkled with excitement when he described the tree lighting ceremony and the torchlight parade. Grant bemoaned how busy he was at the bakery with all the cookie orders for the town's cookie exchange and festival events.

Sugar's phone pinged every few minutes. "Sorry," she said for the umpteenth time. "It's work." After picking at her

The Magic of the Season

plate, eating only the veggies and a few bites of meat, she excused herself from the table and sat by the fire to answer her texts.

Grant helped clear the table, stacking the dishes by the sink where Dottie was scrubbing and Hope was loading the dishwasher. He shook his head and said, "See what I mean, Mom. She's nothing like the Sugar I remember."

"Well, dear, not everything stays the same. People change." said Dottie. "Give her some time to adjust."

"Maybe spending time here at the festival will remind her of Christmas in Silver Falls and soften her," said Hope, pushing the buttons on the dishwasher to start it.

"I wouldn't hold my breath. I think she's been big-city-fied. Any trace of the sweet girl she was in Silver Falls has been erased." Grant sliced the pie and added six plates to a tray. He rolled his eyes and said, "I bet you a bear claw, she won't eat dessert."

Hope chuckled and carried a tray of tea and coffee, along with a hot chocolate, to the living room. Jake and Drew were chatting and petting the dogs while Sugar's fingers flew across the tiny keyboard on her phone.

"How about some pie?" Grant offered a plate to Drew and left one by his mom's chair. Jake took one and sat on the couch next to Drew.

Sugar looked up from her phone and shook her head. "It looks wonderful, but none for me, thanks."

Hope handed her husband a cup of tea and said, "I brewed some tea. Would you like a cup, Sugar?"

She set her phone down and smiled. "That sounds great. I can't seem to stay warm."

Dottie sat and took a bite of pie. "How many orders do you have to fill this week, Sugar?"

"This week, just over a hundred. It increases a bit each week, but the killer is going to be that week before Christmas. Mom has over two hundred boxes planned for the fundraising event, and that's in addition to her regular orders for Christmas."

Sugar's shoulders slumped. "She has a shipment of boxes arriving tomorrow. I've got to get those assembled and make several batches of fudge and caramels between now and Wednesday afternoon." She took another long swallow from her cup. "Speaking of which, I best get home and get started on it."

Hope raised her brows. "I do some work around here for Dottie when we're busy, but I'd be happy to help. I don't know much about making candy, but I'm a quick study."

"That would be terrific. To be honest, I don't know much about it either. Mom always put me to work helping, but I'm not sure how much of it stuck with me. I'd be grateful for anything you can do."

She and Hope made arrangements to meet on Monday morning. Sugar stood and retrieved her coat. "Thank you so much for dinner, Dottie." She met Grant's eyes and then took in Drew and Jake. "And for all your help. I appreciate it. Mom will be so pleased to have the house decorated."

"I hope she does well at the rehab center. I'll try to find a day when I can make a trip to visit her," said Dottie.

"She'd like that. I'm going to run down tomorrow afternoon, but with all the work here, I'm not going to be able to visit often." She wished them all a good evening before opening the door.

Grant followed Sugar outside and made sure she made it down the sidewalk to her Jeep. "Tell Peggy hello for me." She returned his wave as she steered the car out of the driveway.

4

It was still dark when Sugar went downstairs to start her first batch of fudge. Her mother insisted on making small batches, which meant she had to make dozens of batches each day. She also insisted on hairnets. Sugar couldn't stand the itch of the netting. Instead, she plucked her mom's soft red and green fabric hat from the peg on the wall.

She tucked her ponytailed hair inside the hat that resembled a shower cap and washed her hands. She noticed her mom had a red MP3 player on the counter. She pushed the button and was treated to instrumental piano tunes. She started a pot of coffee brewing and got to work, smiling at the framed photos her mom kept above the counter.

There were several of Eddie and Peggy. Their wedding day, outings, early Christmases, the day they bought the house, Peggy holding Sugar as a newborn, and the last one Peggy had taken with Eddie at a summer picnic at Silver Lake.

They both looked so happy and full of life, some twenty-five years ago. Tears filled Sugar's eyes as she scanned the memories displayed before her. She touched her finger to the one with her dad smiling, his arm around Peggy and a view of the lake in the background. "I miss you, Dad," she whispered.

She scanned the opposite wall and saw her mom smiling with Sugar on her graduation day from high school, then from college. Several photos of her mother's beloved black lab, Gypsy, decorated the wall. She had lost Gypsy about five years ago and never got another dog. Pictures of her mom in front of the Christmas tree on Main Street with the mayor, vacation shots of mother and daughter on cruises and tropical beaches, a picture of the two of them on the beach near Sugar's condo, and Peggy smiling when she won the ribbon for the best decorated business one year.

Through watery eyes, Sugar contemplated her mother's life, arranged before her in the photos her mother displayed. Peggy spent more time in this kitchen than she did anywhere else on the planet. She chose to surround herself with memories. With the love of her life, her best furry friend, and her daughter. The daughter who never bothered to visit. Sugar shook her head and focused on the recipe.

As she stirred the butter and chocolate together, the aroma brought back memories of her childhood. Her dad had loved her mom's fudge. Mom had always made it for special friends and colleagues at her dad's office. During Christmas, her mom made batch after batch of the chocolate confection, some with walnuts, others with pecans, and some like rocky road, with marshmallows.

Her dad would tote boxes and platters to work and bring home rave reviews. Each year when the holidays would approach, people would ask Peggy to make them fudge. She used to give it away, but Eddie had encouraged her to set up a business. That had turned out to be a blessing. With the help of their neighbors and friends in Silver Falls, that home-

The Magic of the Season

grown business had supported Sugar and her mother after Eddie died.

Sugar had gotten the feeling everyone bought fudge from her mom out of sympathy for their situation. She knew her Dad had been a beloved fixture at City Hall. He had been the comptroller his entire adult life. The first Christmas after he passed, Peggy had been inundated with orders from everyone at City Hall and the rest of Silver Falls.

It may have started as compassionate purchases, but when Sugar reviewed the order history, it was clear Peggy wasn't selling pity fudge. She was running a booming small business. Sugar finished off the first two batches and slid them into the cooler to chill.

Hope came through the door with a cheerful, "Hellooo, it's just me."

"Hey, Hope, thanks again for volunteering." Sugar turned and took another red apron off the peg. "Here's an apron, and you'll have to wear a hairnet or cover."

"Got it," said Hope, putting on the uniform and washing her hands.

"Coffee's on, if you need any." Sugar went through the process, and they decided Hope would assemble ingredients and get the chilled fudge packaged, while Sugar would handle the actual preparation.

They knocked out several more batches of walnut and pecan before the delivery driver arrived with the candy boxes they needed and an overnight delivery of a power blender. Sugar slit open the cardboard shipping boxes and smiled. "Oh, this is better than the old boxes she always used. These are already assembled and come with a bow and ribbons built into the box." She carried one over to Hope. "I was dreading the time it would take to build them. She must have changed designs."

"This is what she used last year, that's all I know. Dottie could tell you for sure," said Hope.

"It doesn't matter. I'm thrilled to have one less thing to do." She took the box into the kitchen. "Let's see if we can figure out the best system for transferring the fudge into boxes. We'll have to wear gloves."

They filled a few of the boxes, using different ribbon patterns and colors to denote the flavors. Caramels went into a smaller box, so those were easy to distinguish. While they were in the midst of packaging, Drew arrived with takeout bags.

He greeted Hope with a kiss and said, "Thought I'd bring you ladies some lunch." He unpacked containers of soup, salad, and sandwiches from the deli on one of the two petite tables arranged for customers opposite the retail counter.

"That was nice of you. I still haven't gone to the store, so there isn't much here to offer," said Sugar. She eyed the food and said, "Do you know if the salad and soup are organic?"

Drew's forehead creased. "I'm not sure. I know they're delicious." He winked at Sugar.

Sugar dragged another chair over and chose a salad and a container of mushroom soup. Her eyes showed surprise as she took her first bites. "This is quite tasty."

They made easy conversation about the fudge making and packaging processes until Drew had to get back to work. "See you for dinner," he said to Hope, kissing her cheek as he left.

Hope gathered the paper containers and trash. "What time are you heading to visit your mom?"

Sugar looked at her watch. "I'll need to leave in about an hour. Let's put together another couple of batches, and then if you want to stay, you can package what's left in the cooler. I'll get you the order sheets, and you can attach the delivery copy with each order so we're ready to go."

The Magic of the Season

The two worked together, their conversation centered on what they were doing and on Peggy. After sliding the last of the fudge into the cooler, Sugar left Hope with a spare key. "I can't tell you how much I appreciate your help. I feel better having gotten some of this done today."

"It was fun. I'll finish the packaging and come back tomorrow. Wednesday I won't have much time because we'll be busy at the guest house, but I'll have a couple of hours."

Sugar gathered the clothes and books she was taking to her mom, donned her coat, and waved to Hope, thanking her again. "See you in the morning," she said with a smile.

Sugar's alarm beeped at five o'clock. She fumbled in the dark to quiet it and give herself a few more precious minutes. She was exhausted after yesterday. She stayed with her mom until after dinner last night, fighting the urge to sleep as her mom went through all the things Sugar needed to do at the candy shop. Even after hearing how well she and Hope had done with their first batches, Peggy insisted on providing pearls of wisdom. When she started droning on about her temperamental furnace and the electrical outlets, Sugar tuned out her voice.

She made sure her mom was comfortable and had everything she needed, including her favorite channel playing on the television, kissed her goodbye, and made her way to the freeway. Using her phone for directions, she turned into the parking lot of the grocery store she had researched online. She chuckled as she recalled her stroll through what Grant would call a yuppified market. It was going to be her favorite place to shop. She found everything she needed: organic produce, salmon, protein powder, various other staples, and a supply of organic meals from the prepared food counter.

After several minutes, Sugar pried her eyes open and reached for her laptop. Following a solid two hours of answering emails and reviewing projects, she checked the clock and hurried to finish as the first light of the new day filtered into her childhood room.

She scanned the walls while she pondered the last email. Nothing had changed. The shelves held the books she had treasured growing up; her artwork and designs decorated the walls; ribbons she won at art shows still hung on the bulletin board her mother had installed over her desk, whose drawers held all her old art supplies. It was like she had traveled back in time.

She finished her work correspondence, hurried to the shower, and trotted downstairs to start on the fudge. But first, she needed breakfast.

She dumped kale, frozen peaches, frozen mango, ginger, and almond milk into her new blender. After whirling it around for a few minutes, she poured the green mixture into a large glass and drank it down. "Ah, delicious," she said.

She started a fresh pot of coffee and began making rocky road fudge. Hope arrived at nine and donned an apron and hat. The two worked nonstop, pausing only for a quick lunch and to stock the supplies that were delivered by truck. By the time Hope left in the late afternoon, they had all the fudge made for the week's orders, along with over half the caramels wrapped and boxed.

A few minutes after Hope left, Sugar heard the door. "What did you forget?" she hollered from the commercial sink where she was finishing the dishes.

Grant peeked his head around the corner. "Hey, it's me. Smells like chocolate in here." He took another whiff and said, "Heavenly." He contemplated her red apron covered with stains, her hair escaping from the crooked chef's cap, and the weary look in her eyes. "You look like you've been busy. I just came by to check on you."

"Hope just left. We made lots of progress. I couldn't have done it without her."

"Mom wanted me to be sure to invite you to Thanksgiving."

"Aww, that's nice of her. I was going to run into town and visit Mom for a few hours. I doubt I'll have much time to make many trips, so I thought I'd take advantage of being temporarily caught up."

"Mom will hound you until you agree to come. You know that, don't you?" He smiled and helped her steady one of the oversize stainless-steel bowls she had just washed.

"I'll try to stop by when I get back into town. I'm planning to fill more orders and maybe do some of my work from the office. I'm not much on holidays."

He shrugged. "Like I said, it'll be easier if you agree to come. We eat at three. That gives you time to spend the morning with your mom."

She laughed and used her wrist to try to shove a piece of stray hair under her cap. Grant reached for her hair and tucked it behind her ear and under the fabric. His eyes held hers for a second longer than necessary. "There you go." He jerked his hand away with a quick motion and took a step back from the counter.

She studied him out of the corner of her eye. "Tell your mom I'll be there."

He grinned and winked at her. "Smart lady."

She opened the door to the fridge and retrieved the leftover soup and salad from lunch. "I was just going to have a bite of dinner. Care to join me?"

Grant eyed the labels on the containers. "You found your favorite overpriced store. Did you have to fight off any organic, free-range, BMW-driving hipsters?"

She rolled her eyes. "I'm not sure your attitude is worthy of my kale salad and butternut squash soup."

"Um, yeah, I'll pass on both." She poured soup into a bowl and added the rest of her salad to a plate. He sneered and gave her dinner a disgusted look. "I've got to get home and get to bed. I've got a long day of baking starting at three in the morning."

"You must work out. You seem to be in pretty good shape for a guy who eats all those sugary treats you make at the bakery, not to mention all those heavy meals your mom makes."

He stood a little taller. "I don't have time to work out. I like to get outside and hike when I have time, but this time of year, I'm slammed." He grinned and chuckled.

"What's so funny?" She added a fork and a spoon to her tray.

"Ah, nothing." He moved toward the door. "You city girls with your goofy food and yoga obsessions. There's a lot more to life than that." He didn't give her a chance to retort and strode out the door with a quick wave.

She shook her head and muttered, "Like a guy who eats more carbs in a week than I do in a year and has never left this one-horse town would know anything about city life."

Sugar was on her own Wednesday and finished making and wrapping the caramels. She even had time to add a few more batches of fudge to her inventory. The orders for the week were ready for delivery. Her biggest customer was the City of Silver Falls, who ordered dozens of pounds of fudge for the tree lighting ceremony on Friday. Grant's bakery was closed Friday, but he said he would make her deliveries for her.

The Magic of the Season

Between staying up late on Wednesday and getting an early start on Thursday, she was able to catch up on her work from the office. Everyone was taking off for Thanksgiving break and would be out of the office until Monday.

She didn't want to intrude on Hope's time with her family over the holiday weekend, but she could really use her help. While she was thinking about orders, she tapped her phone and put in reminders to order supplies each week.

As she scanned the clipboards and stacks of orders, she shook her head. She had mentioned an online order and invoice system to her mom, but Peggy wanted nothing to do with it. She added a few more things from her mom's room to her tote bag, along with a box of fudge and caramels. Her mom wanted to share with her roommate and asked her to bring some. Sugar suspected she wanted to sample her work and used the roommate as an excuse.

The rehab center was bustling with visitors and decorated for the holiday. She found her mom in the oversized common room with the fireplace, visiting and laughing with the other patients.

Peggy introduced Sugar to her friends and passed around the boxes of candies, making sure to take several for herself. She bit into the chocolate and pecan fudge and closed her eyes. "This is perfect, Sugar. Delicious and so creamy."

Sugar smiled. "I had an excellent teacher. Hope helped me get the orders done this week. She's a hard-worker."

Peggy nodded. "She is a sweet one. You should have seen her last year, running that place for Dottie. She's made such a difference in Drew. He had been so sad since he lost his wife and son so long ago. I didn't think he'd ever be happy again. It's wonderful to see him full of joy and with a family."

Sugar bobbed her head. "The Fishers have always been wonderful friends. Grant's going to deliver orders for me on Friday, and he invited me for Thanksgiving this afternoon."

Peggy's eyebrows arched. "How wonderful. I was hoping you wouldn't be alone today. Grant's such a great guy. He's wonderful to Dottie and has a successful business. He's always willing to help around town. You kids always had so much fun when you were young. You practically lived at their house in the summer."

Sugar smiled. "The lake in their backyard was a huge draw."

Peggy patted her hand. "You know Grant's girlfriend left him last year. Moved away to Boston." She gave her daughter a sly wink.

"Mom," Sugar frowned. "Don't get any crazy ideas. Grant's a nice guy, and he's helping me out. You, actually. That's it."

"Ah, so you're serious about that boy, Darrin?"

"No, I'm not. Darrin is no longer in the picture." A group of young people shuffled into the room. "Thank goodness," whispered Sugar.

One of the staff members introduced the youth group from a local church who had come to sing holiday songs for the patients. After they sang several tunes, the children circled the room wishing everyone a Happy Thanksgiving and presented a decorated cookie to each patient.

The center had planned their big meal for the lunch hour and staff members beckoned everyone to the dining room. Sugar helped her mom maneuver to a table where she met a few more patients.

Sugar visited with everyone until their table was served. "Wow, that's quite the spread," said Sugar, eyeing the heaping plates as they were delivered. The food looked and smelled delicious, not like typical hospital food.

"One of the large casinos in town donates the meal each year. They cater it for us," said the staff member, adding a basket of rolls and butter to the table.

Sugar bent and kissed her mom's cheek, hugging her. "I'll leave you to it. I'm going to get back to Silver Falls. I'll talk to you soon."

"Enjoy your Thanksgiving with the Fishers. Tell Dottie hello and give Grant a hug from me. He'll always be my hero for rescuing me."

5

Sugar picked up four bottles of wine from a grocery store in Reno before she set out for Silver Falls. Hope greeted her at Dottie's front door. Sugar stepped inside and saw Drew and Grant setting up the Christmas tree in the living room.

"Wow, you guys don't waste any time," she said, holding up the wine. "I come bearing gifts and greetings from Mom. She said to tell you all hello."

"Let me take your coat," offered Hope. "Come in and make yourself at home."

Jake was opening all the lids on plastic bins of ornaments and decorations, the dogs were piled in front of a roaring fire, and the fresh scent of pine mingled with the aroma of cinnamon and sugar. It smelled like the Christmases of Sugar's childhood. After hanging the coat, Hope said, "How about something hot to drink? We've got coffee, tea, hot chocolate, or apple cider."

Jake piped up and said, "Hot chocolate for me, Mom."

Sugar laughed and said, "Tea sounds great."

"How about you help us decorate?" said Jake, handing

The Magic of the Season

Sugar an ornament.

"We've got to get the lights on first, buddy," said Grant, turning to face Sugar. "Then we'll put our guest to work."

When Dottie finished in the kitchen, she joined the fun. The ladies sipped their tea while they watched the two brothers wrap the huge tree in hundreds of lights. Sugar hadn't decorated a tree or been part of a family activity centered around a holiday since her youthful days in Silver Falls.

After her dad died, Christmas had been full of sadness and a reminder of happier times lost forever. Her mom tried to continue their traditions, but her heart wasn't in it. Peggy delighted in making her candies and bringing the spirit of Christmas to her customers, but since Eddie had died, she had struggled with the celebration at home.

To escape their memories, the mother and daughter distracted themselves at the holidays. Sugar found excuses to work, and Peggy volunteered at the senior center or the church. The arts center was Peggy's latest passion.

As Sugar helped attach Dottie's collection of ornaments to the branches, she listened to the happy chatter, laughter, and ribbing between Grant and Drew. Each time Dottie chose an ornament, she told them the history of it, where she bought it or who gave it to her, and why it held a special place in her heart. Some ornaments commemorated trips she and Curt had taken to London, Ireland, Scotland, Canada, and several states across America. Others marked milestones or provided fond memories of their pets.

Sugar couldn't help but feel nostalgic while she listened to Dottie's recollections of Christmases past. Eddie had always made Christmas a big deal. He loved the holidays and made sure Sugar's childhood was filled with happy activities and seasonal fun. As she put a pretty hand-blown glass ornament on the tree, one that Curt had bought for Dottie when they were in Germany, a tear trickled down Sugar's cheek. She heard the sorrow in Dottie's voice and knew how she felt.

Hope's phone chimed, and she motioned to Jake and Drew. "It's Tina on video." She led them into the private wing of the house to take the call. Dottie excused herself to check on the turkey.

"Tina is Hope's daughter. She's in college back in Chicago and decided to join her roommate for Thanksgiving this year. She's going to come here for Christmas." Grant explained that last year Drew had arranged for Tina to come to Silver Falls and reunite with Hope. "Their relationship had been strained, but they are working hard to restore it. Jake has adapted to living here and having a new family. It's been harder for Tina."

Sugar adjusted another ornament. "The holidays are a difficult time of year for so many people."

Grant added the capiz star to the top of the tree while Sugar gathered and stacked the ornament boxes and bins. "Looks good, I think we're done." He turned to see if Sugar agreed.

"It's beautiful." She paused, the lights of the tree reflected in her watery eyes. "I haven't had a tree since I left Silver Falls."

"We can remedy that. Your mom always has a tree in the shop. I can help you get one set up in there."

She pondered the idea as she finished her tea. "I didn't want to bother, but I had forgotten how much I always loved the tree."

"It'll be a piece of cake. I'll call Tim over at the tree lot and grab one after we eat. We can put it up tonight."

She shook her head. "I don't want to bother you."

"It's no bother. I like doing it." He took out his cell phone and punched a button. "Tim, hey, it's Grant. Happy Thanksgiving. I have a quick favor to ask."

The Magic of the Season

Dottie came around the corner and said, "Oh, the tree looks wonderful. Thank you for helping, Sugar." She pointed at Grant. "Who's he talking to?"

"Tim at the tree lot. Grant thinks I need to put up a tree and is arranging to get it done after dinner."

Dottie smiled. "He's right. Peggy would never let that slide. She loves having a tree there at the shop."

Sugar laughed. "It's clear I'm powerless to resist in the midst of all of you and your Christmas spirit."

Grant disconnected. "All set. We can swing by tonight and pick one up. Tim says it's on the house for Peggy."

"Aww, that's not necessary," said Sugar. "I'm happy to pay him."

"Everybody loves your mom. It's his way of helping." Grant pointed to the kitchen. "How's the turkey?"

"Just about ready. Come help me with the rest of it, so we can get it on the table," said Dottie.

Dottie tried to find a job for Sugar, but she shook her head at each suggestion. "I'm not good in the kitchen. Mom's candy is the only thing I can make. I eat out mostly."

Sugar poured water into the glasses at each place setting and then took a seat at the huge granite-topped island and watched the mother and son finish preparing the meal. With their fluid movements and easy chatter, it was obvious they cooked together often.

Drew, Hope, and Jake came into the kitchen a few minutes later. "Tina said to tell everyone hello and she can't wait to see you all at Christmas," said Hope.

"That will be here before we know it," said Dottie, handing Drew a bowl of vegetables to put on the table.

"I think we're ready to eat," said Grant, delivering a huge platter of sliced turkey to the table. He followed with the potatoes and gravy.

Dottie pointed to a chair next to Grant's place and said,

"Sugar, you go ahead and sit there." She turned to Jake. "You come sit next to me, sweetie."

They gathered around the heavy wooden table decorated with a festive floral arrangement surrounded by fall leaves and miniature pumpkins. As they passed serving dishes and ate the delicious meal, they talked about the coming weeks and the Festival of Lights. Dottie mentioned the fundraising event Peggy was chairing for the arts program.

"Tell me more about what that involves," said Sugar, loading her plate with more green beans.

"A few years ago, a group got together and took over the old school building. They got some grant money and remodeled it. It's become an important part of the community. They have classes for adults and tons of activities for children and teenagers." Dottie poured more gravy over her plate. "Your mom knew how much art meant to you, especially after you lost your dad. She's been a faithful supporter of the center."

A look of surprise flashed in Sugar's eyes. "She never said much about it."

"This year it's more important than ever. We lost the director at the beginning of the year. We need the fundraiser to keep the center open and to hire a new director. The City of Silver Falls said they can't continue to support it unless the center can attract some donations and more grant funding."

Jake smiled at Dottie and said, "It's so fun. They have all sorts of rooms set up with different activities. I love going there."

"It's been limping by with community volunteers, teachers, and a few donations from local businesses. It's very dear to Peggy's heart." Dottie put a gentle hand on Jake's shoulder. "And to the whole community."

When they finished dinner, Hope and Drew insisted Dottie relax while they took care of all the dishes. Grant

The Magic of the Season

turned to Sugar and gestured toward the door. "How about we go get that tree of yours decorated, and then we'll come back for pie?" He wiggled his brows at his mom.

"I hate to eat and run. I'm happy to help with the clean-up duties," said Sugar.

"Nonsense. You two go on. Hope and Drew can handle it," said Dottie. "Jake can help clear the table and then read me a story while we wait for dessert."

Grant held Sugar's coat, and she slipped into it. "My truck's out back."

He drove to town and parked alongside the bakery, on the side street. Grant had let Tim put up some fencing and create a makeshift tree lot on the wide sidewalk next to the bakery. He found the key on his ring and unlocked the heavy padlock that held the fencing together.

"Okay, time to choose a tree." Grant stood several up so she could inspect them.

"I haven't picked out a tree in years. Which one do you like?"

He plucked a Douglas fir from the stack. "This one has a great shape."

She nodded and walked around it to look at it from all angles. "It's perfect."

He loaded it into the truck and reattached the lock. He rubbed his gloved hands together. "It's getting cold. Let's get moving."

He drove to the end of Main Street and parked in front of Peggy's house. While Sugar unlocked the door, he hefted the tree down the walkway and leaned it against the house on the porch. "Let's find the stand and make sure we have a spot for it before I take it inside."

They rummaged in the storage room and uncovered boxes of ornaments and the tree stand, along with a stepladder. They rearranged the tables and chairs in the customer area and made room for the tree in front of the window. Sugar held the door open while Grant muscled the tree inside and set it in the stand.

"Do you want to hold it, and I'll get down there and tighten the screws?" he asked.

She nodded and reached inside the thick branches to hold the trunk while Grant slid under the tree. A few minutes later he emerged. "Okay, looks straight. Just make sure you keep this filled with water. We don't want it to dry out."

While Grant worked on gathering enough strings of lights, she fetched a pitcher and made sure the reservoir was full. He started wrapping the tree with lights and passed them off to her to string around the other side. She took great care to keep the lights spaced evenly and rearranged Grant's to match.

"For someone who doesn't do trees, you sure are picky," joked Grant.

Sugar smirked and kept stringing the lights. "It's my job to be finicky about details. I can't help it."

"I smell coffee," said Grant.

"I started some brewing when I was in the kitchen. I'm freezing," she said.

Grant left the lights in her capable hands. "I'll bring you back a cup."

"No sugar, I take mine black," she said.

He returned and set her cup on the table nearest her and cradled his in his hands. "Looks nice. Time for the stepladder." He took another sip before setting his cup down. He positioned the ladder close to the tree. "Do you want me to do the high part?"

"I can do it," she said, climbing onto the first step. She wobbled a bit, and he reached out and steadied her around the waist.

"You got it?" He kept his hand at the small of her back.

The Magic of the Season

She laughed. "I think so, but no guarantees."

He stood close by and kept his hand in place. "It looks great. Like a professional did it." She stepped down from the ladder to admire her handiwork and took a sip from her cup.

"Ready for ornaments?" Grant opened the first box. "Are there rules, or can I just put some on the tree?"

"You can put them on." She arched her brows and added, "But I reserve the right to relocate them."

As they worked together, she asked him more about the old school building and the fundraiser. "I've been thinking about how to gather some interest and raise enough money so the center is viable. I think we need some sponsors."

"All the businesses in Silver Falls have donated quite a bit already. We get hit up all the time for local stuff. I don't know that they have much more to give."

She nodded. "I mean big sponsors. I'm thinking of a few of our major clients at the advertising firm." She moved a couple of the ornaments he had placed. "I also want to use the Internet to get more people involved and excited. Make it easy to donate even if someone is out of the area. Advertise the event and try to make it go viral. I need to think about it a bit."

"For the girl who said she wasn't going to do it, sounds like you've already been doing more than some thinking."

She chose some more ornaments from the box. "What Dottie said about my mom recognizing the importance of art for me struck a nerve." She attached a vintage Santa to a branch. "Art saved me. It let me escape from the cloud I was living under after my dad died. It gave me a path forward and the career I have today. I want to make sure it's available to others."

Grant opened another box of ornaments. "It's popular with all age groups. They've done a good job of catering to the entire community. Mom's taken some classes there, and

Jake loves it. I think they even have family nights because Drew went with Hope and Jake to something."

"I forgot what a small town was like," she said, climbing up the ladder to add some miniature ornaments to the upper part of the tree. "That sense of community and belonging isn't there for me in Santa Monica."

"I couldn't do a big city. I love it here. It can be a little overwhelming when it seems like everyone knows everything about you, like last year when Lisa and I broke up. Everyone that came into the bakery had to tell me how sorry they were. It went on and on and made me nuts." He handed her a few more ornaments.

"I haven't had anything resembling a boyfriend for years. My dates are like solar eclipses—once or twice a year and short-lived."

Grant chuckled. "Lisa and I were together for several years. I thought she was the one."

"What happened?" She gasped and added, "Sorry, you don't have to tell me. It's none of my business."

"It's okay. Everybody else knows." He took a deep breath and explained that Lisa hadn't told him she had applied for a job in Boston. She ended up getting the job and expected Grant to move across the country with her. "She wanted more. Her life here in Silver Falls wasn't enough. I wasn't enough."

"I'm sorry, Grant. I'm sure that was devastating after such a long relationship." She shrugged. "I've never been lucky enough to have someone in my life for that long. I tend to concentrate on work and building my career. It doesn't leave much time for a personal life." She turned to face him. "Even though she's gone, I'd say you were lucky to have her."

He frowned. "That's a different way of looking at it. It took me a long time to get over it. Honestly, I'm not sure I'm over her yet, but at least it's not on my mind all the time. I've always got plenty to do at the bakery or around town. It's not easy to date in Silver Falls, so I've been spending most of my free time with family."

She inspected her work and said, "You have a wonderful family. Like I said, lucky guy."

He opened a decorative box inside the bin of ornaments. "Oh, this looks like the topper. Can you do it, or do you want me to climb up there?"

She looked at the angel he held and brought her hand to her throat. "Oh, wow, I haven't seen her in years. That belonged to my grandmother. My dad's mom." With a gentle hand, she took the delicate angel from the tissue. "I think I can reach."

She fluffed the white and gold dress with ornate ribbons, soft feathers, and delicate pearls. With great care, she placed the angel, which resembled an antique doll, on top of the tree. She made a couple of minor adjustments and stepped down from the ladder.

"It looks terrific," said Grant. "Just like Peggy would have done." He turned to Sugar and noticed tears on her cheeks. "Are you okay?"

She nodded. "Too many memories."

"I'll get these boxes put away," he offered, leaving her alone to admire the tree. When he returned from the storage room, she was sitting at one of the tables, using a napkin to blot her eyes.

He placed his hand on her shoulder. "You ready? We better get back to the house. They'll be eager for pie. Not to mention we always watch a movie with dessert. It's one of Dad's traditions."

She smiled and took the hand he offered. As he opened the passenger door for her, she gripped his hand in hers. "Thanks for doing this tonight. I didn't want the tree, but I think I needed it."

6

Sugar started bright and early Friday morning and had several batches of fudge made by the time Hope arrived to help. Grant packed all her outgoing orders into his bakery van and promised to have them delivered by the end of the day. He was also willing to let customers pick up their candy orders at his bakery so Sugar could work uninterrupted. Sugar posted a sign to let customers know of the changes.

By the time Hope and Sugar hung up their aprons, they had boxes of fudge stacked in the cooler and hundreds of wrapped caramels boxed on the counter. "Thanks again for all your help, Hope. I really need to pay you for your time," said Sugar.

Hope shook her head. "It's not a big deal. Jake is spending time with Drew today. The veterinary office is closed, so he's got the time off. They're up on the hill sledding today, enjoying some bonding time."

"I'm sure they're having fun. That was always a popular place to be in the winter when I was growing up here."

Hope slipped into her coat. "So, we'll meet you at the tree lighting tonight? Don't forget chili at Dottie's afterward."

"I'll be there." She looked at her watch. "I'm meeting a guy from the city for a tour of the arts center, but I'll be there. I'm working on ideas for the fundraiser and wanted to get a look at the place."

"We'll save you a spot at the tree," said Hope, giving Sugar a quick hug.

Sugar bundled up in her warmest clothes and drove through town, skirting Main Street, which was closed off for the evening's activities. The old school, a beautiful Beaux Arts style building, with huge columns at the top of the stairs leading to the entrance, stood above a wide grassy area. It was a massive building, taking up the whole block across from the park. Sugar hadn't attended school there, but her mother had. It held a special place in the hearts of the people of Silver Falls.

It was decked out in Christmas lights with beautiful, fresh wreaths hung on the double doors of the entrance. She opened the door to the lobby. It had the traditional black-and-white tiles used in so many buildings of the same era. She stepped into the main building and saw a Christmas tree in the corner, its lights reflected in the polished wooden flooring.

"Hello there. You must be Peggy's daughter, Madison?" said a gray-haired man coming around the corner. "I'm Clint London. We spoke on the phone."

"Yes," she said, shaking his hand. "Nice to meet you, Mr. London and you can call me Sugar. Everyone here does."

"I'll show you the highlights and leave you with a key so you can do whatever you need to do for the fundraising event. Your mom has been so supportive of our endeavor. I'm so sorry about her accident."

He led her through the restored classrooms that served as workshop areas, studios, and teaching space. The halls were lined with artwork from the participants. Every type of art was represented, whether it be traditional painting, ceramics, photography, or fabric arts, along with knitted and crocheted pieces. Beautiful stained-glass pieces hung in a window, reflecting the Christmas lights outside. There was even a display of poetry and short stories crafted by teenagers in Silver Falls.

A large classroom was outfitted with mirrored walls and a wooden barre along the longest wall. "They do dance classes too?" she asked.

Mr. London nodded. "Silver Falls is too small to support individual businesses like a dance studio, so the Silver Falls Arts Center provides an umbrella where all interests can be explored. It's a great way for people of all ages to try different art forms."

He led her to a door off a hallway that led to the stage, the centerpiece of the old auditorium. Beautiful red curtains draped the sides of the polished wooden stage. "We've been doing a couple of plays each year. Two local teachers spearhead that endeavor, and they are always well attended."

"Wow, this is all wonderful. I would have loved to have had this around when I was growing up here. It's terrific."

Mr. London gave her a sad smile. "Since we lost our director, volunteers and some of us from the city have been coordinating things to keep the doors open, but if we don't get a windfall, it's not going to be possible to keep this place going." He shook his head. "It's a real shame."

"How much do we need?"

He lowered his voice and uttered a number with more zeros than Sugar had anticipated.

"Wow. I can't imagine raising that much in a month. Is there any wiggle room?"

"I'm afraid not. We're running on borrowed time now. The city has to shut it down on December thirty-first if we don't have the funds."

The Magic of the Season

He led her upstairs where more classrooms housed activities for the younger artists. Tissue paper snowflakes and colorful Christmas trees decorated the walls. He gave her a quick tour of the basement area, which was mostly used for the storage of supplies. However, it also contained a kitchen area and plenty of open space, as well as all the mechanical systems for the building. Sugar took it all in, her mind churning with ideas.

Mr. London handed her a keyring. "This key works on all the doors, but you'll only have to worry about locking the front door tonight. I'll come back after the tree lighting to set the alarm. Feel free to explore. If you need anything, give me a call. I'm happy to help." He led her back upstairs. He pointed to a door off the lobby. "This is the office. Feel free to use the desk, phone, whatever you need."

"Thank you. I've got some ideas but seeing this helps." She waved to him and continued wandering through the main level. She eyed the artwork on the walls and found more stashed in each of the classrooms. Beading, leatherwork, wood carvings and bowls, even some metal sculptures lined the shelves in one workshop.

She used her phone and snapped dozens of photos. Lingering at the stairs leading down to the audience area in front of the stage, she considered the space. When she was younger, she had heard tales from some of the old-timers who recounted their time at the school. The auditorium space had been used for every type of activity. Basketball games, band concerts, town meetings, plays, and school dances had all taken place in what had become known as "the pit". Two small balcony areas on each side of the auditorium could be accessed from the hallway surrounding it.

Leaning against one of the archways that circled the center of the main floor, she pictured it trimmed for the season. Seeds of ideas started to sprout as she contemplated what could be done to save the center.

She locked the door and left her Jeep in the parking lot, choosing to walk through the park to Main Street. She passed by the gazebo, adorned with hundreds of lights, and smiled at a man wearing a top hat waiting by his horse-drawn carriage.

Everyone greeted Sugar with a smile or holiday greeting. As she neared Main Street, she walked by a cart with hot beverages and cookies. "How about a cup of cocoa?" asked the man standing behind the cart.

"No. Thank you, though." She smiled and kept moving toward the tree where it looked like the entire population of Silver Falls was huddled. Amid the buzz of conversation and excitement, a choir sang carols. She kept her eyes open for Grant or Drew, hoping to spot their heads above the crowd.

She moved to the side of the street Grant's bakery was on and continued her search. She heard Grant's voice yell, "Sugar, over here." She saw him waving from a spot near the front of the crowd.

She wriggled through everyone just in time to watch the mayor take the stage. He thanked everyone for coming, talked about all the festivities planned for the Festival of Lights, and then got the crowd counting down to the lighting of the tree.

When the crowd shouted, "Three-two-one," he pushed the plunger on a red box, and the tree came to life. Thousands of lights twinkled as everyone oohed and aahed at the impressive display. The choir burst into song as the audience cheered. All the trees lining Main Street were wrapped in strands of white lights. Colorful lights gleamed from every storefront along the sidewalks.

As she took in the postcard-worthy scene, Sugar's eyes went wide. She grabbed Grant's arm with her gloved hand. "I can't believe this. It's so much grander than what I remember."

He laughed and smiled, taking her hand in his. "There's more to come."

Fireworks began to explode above the tree and lit up the dark velvet sky with bursts of light. It wasn't snowing, but snow machines installed on the old lamp posts began sending out soft flakes of white snow, showering the merry-makers surrounding the tree.

It was magical. Sugar stood in awe, watching the dancing embers of the fireworks. She took out her phone and captured several photos of the tree with the fireworks above it. Jake was going crazy, cheering at every new explosion.

As she was taking in the last torrent of colors twinkling and fizzling against the night sky, she heard the crowd cheering. The man of the hour had arrived. Santa took his seat in a red velvet chair, and the children squealed with delight.

Sugar stood next to Grant and watched as Jake inched closer to the front of the line and Santa's elf. Santa took his time with each child, listening and laughing, posing for photos. Parents and grandparents took dozens of photos as they watched the smiling faces of the little ones perched on Santa's lap.

Santa's elves gave everyone candy canes, and tables and carts with hot drinks and cookies were stationed throughout the street. The old theater was running a free showing of "It's a Wonderful Life", and stores were open for holiday shoppers.

After Hope and Dottie took several photos of Jake, he emerged from the red carpet lined exit pathway sporting a huge grin. Dottie reached for Sugar's arm. "Don't you run away. Come on over to the house. Chili and lots of cookies."

"I'll be there. I've got to run back to pick up my car at the arts center."

"Grant can drive you. It's freezing," said Dottie, looking at her son.

"Sure. I've got my van at the bakery."

Jake was chattering nonstop about his visit with Santa, the fireworks, and the lights. He was between Drew and Hope, holding their hands, as they made their way down the street.

"I'm almost as excited as Jake. I still can't believe our hometown tree lighting morphed into this extravaganza." Sugar turned to take another look at the tree.

Grant stood beside her. "It's one of my favorite things about Silver Falls. This time of year is the best time to live here. For a girl who claims not to celebrate Christmas, it seems we're winning you over."

She turned to meet his gaze. "I used to love Christmas. With Mom and Dad, it was always special and fun. But it's become easier to ignore it because it reminds me of all I've lost. How empty my life is. How much I'm missing. But this has been more than I expected. It's almost magical."

"Wait until you see the torchlight parade down the mountain next weekend. It'll blow you away." He took her hand and led her to the bakery. "I need to run by City Hall. I promised I'd make an appearance since they're hosting an open house and I supplied all the goodies."

He drove the few blocks and snagged one of the few parking spots close to the building. He led the way through the courtyard which was outfitted with festive decorations. Every bush and tree had been draped in lights. Grant held the door for her, and she said, "Wow, this is beautiful."

Strands of white lights were draped from the ceiling, forming a canopy of twinkling illumination over the narrow hallway that ran the length of the building. Human sized nutcracker soldiers flanked the doorways, a tree stood near

The Magic of the Season

the mayor's office, and tables of cookies, snacks, and hot beverages were around every corner.

"Hey, Grant," said several of the staffers in the hallway. Others echoed "Great cookies." Grant shook hands with everyone and made his way to the mayor's office at the end of the hallway.

Mayor Douglas greeted Grant with a hearty handshake and clap on the shoulder. "Thanks once again, Grant. Your cookies and treats are always the hit of the evening here."

"Happy to do it." He turned to Sugar. "This is Peggy White's daughter, Sugar. She's been taking over the candy shop while her mom's recuperating."

She gave Grant a sideways look and said, "My name is actually Madison. Sugar's my nickname, which I can't seem to shake," she added with a grin.

The mayor smiled and said, "We all know ya by Sugar. Your mom's always talking about you. So glad you're here to help out and spend Christmas in Silver Falls. Clint tells me you're getting up to speed on the arts center. I wish you luck, young lady."

"I think I'll need more than luck. I wasn't prepared for the amount Mr. London said they need," she said.

"It's a wonderful facility and program. We've been carrying it this year, but we've reached the limit, I'm afraid. If you need any manpower or help, let me know. We'll do all that we can." He motioned to the tables set up in the foyer. "You two help yourselves to some snacks. I've got to go greet some others. Merry Christmas."

They said their goodbyes, and Grant led her on a tour through the building, checking the supplies of cookies and noting several empty trays as they went. "Looks like they were popular."

"Do you have to collect the trays?" she asked.

"Nah, I'll get them next week. The staff usually keeps the

leftovers and leaves the trays for me." He held the side door open for her.

They made their way to the parking lot, as people on the sidewalk continued to stop and greet Grant. He opened the passenger door for her. "Sounds like your mom bit off quite the project with the fundraiser."

"I took a look at the old school today, and I've got some ideas. I'll have to talk to Mom and find out what she was planning, but I'm not sure it's realistic to think we can raise the funds required."

"It's the season of miracles. Maybe some Silver Falls magic will do the trick."

Despite her nickname, Sugar tried to avoid the sweet stuff as much as possible, but Dottie insisted she sample Grant's cookies after her bowl of chili. He was getting ready for the cookie exchange that would take place in two weeks and had been baking his old favorites and testing a few new recipes.

Sugar acquiesced and took several small bites of the cookies. They were attractive and so delicious, but the sugar overload made her unable to sleep. She stayed up into the early hours of the morning Saturday, sketching concepts and making lists for the fundraiser.

The strong relationships she had built over her career would come in handy for several of her ideas. She composed emails to the clients she knew had ties to the arts and community-minded organizations and a few others she knew would be willing to help.

She slept for only a few hours before it was time to begin her work in the kitchen. Hope wouldn't be able to come back until Monday, so she was on her own for the next two days.

After an extra-large green smoothie and some coffee, she

powered through batch after batch of fudge. By late afternoon, she was exhausted. She scanned through the stack of orders she had to complete, breathing a sigh of relief when she added up the batches in her head.

"This is doable." She double-checked the boxes in the cooler before she went upstairs, doing the math in her head. "If I can keep up this pace, it'll work."

She fell into bed and was asleep the moment her head hit the pillow.

Sunday morning, she watered the Christmas tree while her coffee brewed. Close to lunch, she heard a loud knock on the door. She smiled when she saw Grant waving through the window.

"How's it going?" he asked, holding two cups from the bakery. "I brought you a coffee. Thought you might need one."

She smiled and took the cup. "Thank you, come in."

He followed her into the kitchen and hung his coat. "You've been a busy bee."

"I'm getting there. Making progress." She slid a batch into the cooler to chill. "You making deliveries and handling the walk-ins at the bakery has been a huge help. I couldn't have done all this and tried to run the counter as well. I know Mom usually found a high school student to help her in the afternoon, but I don't have the energy to train and supervise someone."

"Happy to help. Drew and Hope took Mom down to Reno today to visit your mom. They're doing some shopping, so she'll be able to spend the day with her."

"Oh, she'll love that. I'm going to call her tonight. I feel bad, but I don't have the time to take off and go see her right now. I'm hoping she'll be home for Christmas Eve. It will break her heart if she's still in that place. I know she's working extra hard to get out." She carried bowls to the sink and began washing them.

"She's a tough lady. My money's on her." He grabbed a towel and began drying the clean dishes.

"I was about to heat up some soup. Would you like some?"

He wrinkled his nose. "It's probably grass clippings and granola or something, right?"

She shook her head. "It's tomato and zucchini today."

"That's probably not horrible, but I'm on my way to Mom's. Leftover chili sounds better." He took his coat from the hook. "Don't forget the torchlight parade in a week. We're all going, and you're welcome to join us. You won't want to miss it."

"Sounds great, but I have one condition. I get to treat all of you to dinner afterward."

Panic flashed in his eyes. "Uh, you don't have to do that."

"Don't worry, I meant a restaurant. Not my cooking." She laughed.

"In that case, we accept." He grinned and said, "See ya later."

After lunch, Sugar boxed the chilled fudge and started on the batches for the afternoon. As she worked, she contemplated the arts center and tried to narrow down her ideas. After finishing the chocolates, she had time for a batch of caramels. Once they were wrapped and boxed, she called it a day and went upstairs.

She was anxious for Monday morning, once the holiday weekend was over, when she was hoping for responses to her emails. When she was snuggled in her bed with her laptop, she put in a call to her mom.

Sugar asked her for some details about the party she planned for Christmas Eve. After getting sidetracked with updates on her surprise visit with Dottie, Peggy confessed that she hadn't had time to plan much and knew Sugar would have some wonderful ideas. Sugar let out a long breath and listened as her mom complained about one of the staff members who wasn't very nice to the patients and the lack of good quality snacks. Sugar refocused her mom on her progress and the fun day she had enjoyed with her friend before wishing her a good night.

Sugar turned her attention back to her laptop. Her fingers flew over the keys as she made lists, created a website, and worked with some design software. She smiled when she viewed her finished product and closed the lid on her laptop.

7

Monday morning, Sugar's office in California was back in full swing, and her phone chimed nonstop. She dealt with some work issues and checked her email before heading downstairs to start her day.

Her eyes brightened when she saw several responses to her requests for help. All the clients she had approached offered their support. She sent a flurry of replies with attachments and trotted down the stairs to the kitchen, her steps lighter with a sense of accomplishment.

With Hope's help, she was able to get all the orders for the week completed by Thursday. She'd been working on the fundraiser in the evenings and every spare minute she could capture during the day. With her work done for the week, she would have Friday to concentrate on the arts center.

Dottie had sent a message via Hope inviting Sugar to dinner. She changed clothes, gathered her laptop and the folder with the fundraising information, and made her way to Dottie's, taking Main Street to get a glimpse of the cheerful lights and decorations.

She noticed Grant's truck was parked in the driveway

when she arrived. He met her at the door and welcomed her, with the help of all five dogs. Once she had been sniffed and deemed acceptable, the dogs wandered off to sit in front of the fire. Grant took her coat, but she held onto her oversized tote bag.

Hope and Jake were in the kitchen visiting with Dottie, and Drew was still at work. "So glad you came, Sugar," said Dottie from behind the sink. "We're waiting on Drew, so help yourself to something hot to drink and make yourself comfortable by the fire."

"I've got some ideas for the fundraiser I was hoping to run by all of you. I'd like to get your opinions." She took the cup of tea Grant offered.

"Well, grab a chair here at the island and tell us all about it," said Dottie.

Sugar unearthed her laptop and turned it on while she took a few pages from her folder. "I've got the ball rolling with some of my clients from work. Several of them are good about helping nonprofits, and they've all been more than receptive."

She showed them a mockup of a calendar she had designed featuring a variety of artwork from the center. Each month showcased a piece made by someone in Silver Falls, along with the artist's name. "One of the companies offered to print all of these and ship them here so we could sell them."

"That looks great. So professional," said Hope.

Sugar's eyes widened with excitement. "And one hundred percent profit for us. Instead of asking for a flat-out donation, we can sell them. It won't make a ton, but I can imagine lots of relatives buying them because they feature artwork by their grandkids or nieces and nephews. My client will even pay to ship the calendars if folks buy them from out of town."

"That sounds terrific," said Dottie.

"I've also got a mega donor. It's a company that makes skis and snowboards. They're excited about it and are running an online promotion for us. They'll be donating a portion of the proceeds from the sale of their products this month. There's a tie-in with our ski resort, and it'll be huge," said Sugar, her eyebrows arched.

She took a breath and continued. "I've got a crowdfunding campaign set up online. That means we can get donations from everywhere. I've described the need and showcased some photos of the art work, the classes, and the beautiful town. It makes it simple for anyone here or around the world to donate. We already have some donations, and I haven't even advertised it."

Her eyes sparkled with enthusiasm. "I also have a multi-national client, and one of their subsidiaries is an art supply company. They're willing to donate all the center's supplies for two years, and they're also making a five-figure donation. Another one of my clients is the parent company for several chain restaurants. They've offered to do an Evening for the Arts in all their restaurants and donate a portion of their sales to several programs, including ours."

"Wow, that's impressive," said Grant. "I can't believe you've got all this done this week."

Sugar held up a finger. "There's more. I've worked up some posters and signs and would like to approach local businesses about possibly adding on a donation with their regular purchases. For instance, at the bakery, you could say get a dozen pastries for the normal price or get a dozen pastries and sponsor a student at the art center for a month for a higher price. That way, businesses aren't being asked to carry the load, only to help spread the word and give people an easy way to donate. The big donors are saving us right now, but it's important the community be involved. I want to garner their support so it becomes a habit."

"Makes sense. It's something everybody loves. I just think they couldn't figure out a way to squeeze any more support from the locals." Grant looked at Sugar's poster and flyer designs. "I think this will work. This time of year, we get so many tourists, especially at the ski resorts, restaurants, gas stations, all the shops on Main Street for the festival, even here at Mom's guest house. I can see them getting in the spirit and supporting the cause," said Grant.

"I was hoping some of the kids might volunteer to do gift wrapping for people. They could set up some booths around town to make it convenient and wrap presents for donations and to spread the word about our fundraiser. One other idea I had was for a couple of trivia nights at the local tavern. We could charge a registration fee that would go toward the arts center and have prizes for the winners. Is the Tipsy Moose still the only bar in town?" asked Sugar.

Grant laughed. "There are a couple of others, but they aren't very busy. The Moose is your best bet. Danny runs it, he's a good guy. I can help you talk to him. Thursday and Friday nights would be busy with tourists. Saturdays he's got pool and dart tournaments."

Sugar made a checkmark next to her list. "Okay, so that about covers it, except for the gala."

"Gala, that sounds elegant," said Hope.

"I thought it would be fun to have a fancy Christmas Eve party at the school." She flipped over the sketches she had done of the pit decorated for the event. "The art supply company and the ski company have agreed to cover the costs for the gala. We'll feature them as the sponsors and highlight everything they're doing to support the center. I'd like to see the gala become an annual affair. Not at Christmas, there's too much going on, but maybe in the spring or fall. With that in mind, I'd like to do a silent auction, which will involve soliciting some prizes from local businesses, and I want to have some local artists donate some of their work."

She sipped her tea while the others perused her sketches. "I've found some grants we can apply for and will work with Mr. London to see if the city can help with those. I'm trying to figure out a way to sustain the center for the future, not just solve this current crisis."

Dottie looked up from the drawings and beamed. "All I can say is Silver Falls is lucky to have you, sweetie. Your work is unbelievable. Everyone is going to be thrilled."

"You think so?" asked Sugar. "I know it's a lot to take in, but with all the sponsors and help, I think we can do it." She turned to look at Grant. "The mayor and Mr. London said they'd do anything to help."

He chuckled. "I doubt they expected all this, but I think they'll be thrilled. It looks like you're going to set the place up for success. With all this, the center will have more than enough to keep it going."

"That's the plan. This is our big push to get us in the black and build up a reserve so we can make sure the center stays open for everyone in the years to come."

The sound of five dogs' nails on the floors hurrying to the back door announced Drew's arrival. "Let's get dinner on the table," said Dottie, taking a huge pan out of the oven. "We can show him your plans."

While they ate, they continued to hash out Sugar's ideas. Drew agreed with the others and thought the ideas were creative and solid. "I'm going to meet with Mr. London tomorrow and explain everything," said Sugar. "I'm counting on him spearheading the logistics for the gala event."

Drew rattled off several businesses in town and said, "I can talk to all of them and get them involved. You can count us in at the vet clinic too." Drew volunteered to contact the local Elk's Club and coordinate them handling the bar at the gala.

"I thought I'd give Mom the job of contacting some of her business friends and getting them onboard. That way she'll feel like she's contributing."

Grant helped himself to another serving of potatoes. "See if Mr. London can print your flyers up for the local businesses. They've got a fancy copier at City Hall. We could get to work distributing them right away."

"I'll go see him first thing tomorrow." Sugar penned a note in her folder. "The sponsors are shipping the gala decorations to me. They'll be here this week so I can get started on the design." She turned to Hope. "Do you think we could wrangle some help from students and volunteers over the weekend?"

"I'll send out the word. I can work on coordinating the wrapping stations. That's a fun idea and a great way for the kids to be involved. As far as the artwork, I'm sure I can get folks to help, especially when they know more about the gala." Hope looked at her husband. "We'll be there for sure."

Sugar smiled. "I've got everything set up online. I built a website for the center and added a donation button. It'll go live tomorrow. I've got a "call for volunteers" email drafted. I don't have their names. I'll send it to you, and you can customize it and send it out." She made a few more notes in her folder. "This is all starting to come together."

"How about fresh berry cobbler and some ice cream for dessert?" Dottie winked at Jake.

Sugar held up her hand. "I'm going to pass on even a bite of dessert tonight. I've got to be careful on the sweets."

"You might be in the wrong house," Drew said with a chuckle.

Dottie smiled at her son. "This time of year, Silver Falls is all about the taste of Christmas and the magic of the season."

"I'm counting on that magic." Sugar reached for Dottie's hand. "We need it to make all of this work."

8

After Grant stopped by the Sugar Shop early Friday morning and loaded all the orders, Sugar made a quick stop at the mercantile to pick up a space heater and a power strip. She was tired of freezing and not having enough outlets to plug in her electronics.

Once at the school, she chose some of the artwork she had discovered on her tour and began positioning it around the auditorium to showcase the shiniest examples of what they offered.

Her phone chimed a few minutes before eight o'clock, reminding her to get to City Hall. It only took a few minutes to make the drive. She remembered where Mr. London's office was from the tour Grant gave her.

He was standing in the doorway when she arrived. "Mr. London, I was hoping you had a few minutes this morning."

"Come right in, Sugar." She took the cup of coffee he offered, hoping to warm her hands. She went through her plans with him, let him view the mockup of the calendar, showed him the flyers she wanted to post around Silver Falls, and solicited his help with the logistics for the gala.

She finished her presentation and sat back in her chair. He focused on the sketches and flyers on his desk for several minutes. "This is remarkable. I can't believe you've secured all these donations so quickly. It's wonderful news." He took another look at the designs. "I'll get these copied right away. I'll call Ryan, he's our point person for handling all the logistics, and you can work directly with him to get everything set up like you want it." He took the flyers and made his way to the door.

He turned around and smiled at Sugar. "The mayor is going to be thrilled. I'll be right back." He hurried down the hall, giving instructions to one of the secretaries.

Sugar used the time to check the tracking information on the supplies for the gala. They were due to arrive before noon and would be delivered directly to the school. She scrolled through her work emails and corresponded with her assistant.

A few minutes later, Mr. London returned with a young dark-haired man with a crooked smile he introduced as Ryan. "Ryan and his team will be at your disposal. We ran into the mayor in the hall and gave him a quick update. He's delighted and said he'll be at the gala."

Ryan handed her a business card. "My cell phone number is on the back. I've got it with me all the time, so call if you need anything."

Sugar slipped the card in her purse. "I'm heading back to the school now. The decorations are arriving this morning. Are you able to stop by so we can go over things?"

They made plans for Ryan to visit the school after lunch. A secretary came through the door and set a tall stack of flyers on the table. Mr. London patted the stack and said, "We've got some interns who can help distribute these throughout Silver Falls. The mayor loves the calendar and said he'll make sure they're stocked for sale all over town. I'll

The Magic of the Season

get the event added to our website and promote it at all of our holiday events."

"Sounds terrific." Sugar grabbed a stack of flyers. "We're going to visit some businesses, and Mom is going to make some calls. Between all of us, we'll get the word out. As soon as the calendars arrive, I'll drop some off to you. Should be early next week."

On her way back to the school, she dropped off some flyers with Drew's receptionist at the vet clinic. Once at the school, she taped some flyers to the windows of the entrance doors and reviewed her sketches of the auditorium, tweaking them here and there.

The delivery driver arrived and carted box after box into the school. He was nice enough to stack them near the old auditorium to save her the trouble. She dug into the boxes and began organizing thousands of lights, ornaments, decorative branches, trees, vases, candles, ribbons, and fabric.

Ryan arrived with a young woman he introduced as Annie. She shook hands with Sugar and handed her a business card. "I help coordinate events for the City of Silver Falls and will be assisting Ryan." Annie opened a notebook.

Sugar took the card and nodded. "The theme I've chosen is The Magic of the Season. Silver Falls is the epitome of Christmas, and I've been reminded of how magical it can be here." Sugar showed them the decorations and supplies and explained how she wanted the space arranged, the numbers and types of tables and chairs, and the overall look she was hoping to achieve. Annie nodded her head several times as she jotted notes.

"I'm planning on having appetizer stations and a no-host bar, as well as festive punch and non-alcoholic beverages." Sugar pointed out the areas. "I'm going to use local restaurants and service clubs for all of that."

Sugar consulted her notes. "I've got to stop by the florist

and the nursery for some of our other needs. We'll use the stage for the musical guests. We'll need to make sure the sound system is working and have a microphone we can use." Sugar ran her finger down her list.

"I left the long boxes of red carpeting out in the foyer area. I would like those used for the entrance and to create a path up the stairs." She flipped to the exterior sketch she had done.

"We should have volunteers here this weekend to help get the classrooms ready and the rest of our artwork hung on the walls surrounding this main auditorium area. We've only got three weeks to pull this together, and with my mom's condition, I have to spend most of my time at the Sugar Shop. I appreciate all the help in getting this done."

Ryan nodded. "We're happy to help. You can count on us; don't worry about a thing. We will probably hold off on most of this until the week of the event. We've got some other projects we're working on for the festival, but the last week will be our slowest time."

"Perfect. I don't want anyone to see it early, so we'll make sure all of our work is done in the coming two weeks and leave you free to work that final week so we can keep it under wraps. I'll coordinate deliveries of anything else with you," said Sugar. She made sure they had her cell phone number before they left.

She checked the time and hurried down the street to meet the pastor of Silver Falls Community Church. She admired the beautiful stone building with its colorful stained-glass windows, tall bell tower, and steeple. She opened the heavy wooden doors and found Pastor Dunmore in his office.

After she introduced herself, he asked about Peggy. "She's making progress. I'm hopeful she'll be home by Christmas Eve." She handed him a flyer and said, "I'm taking over her fundraising project for the arts center. I've got a gala planned

The Magic of the Season

for that evening. I know you're having your Christmas Eve candlelight service that evening at eleven o'clock. We'll be wrapping up the event shortly before then and will be encouraging people to light a candle and walk over to the church for your service. I'm hoping you and Mrs. Dunmore will attend the gala."

He beamed with delight. "That sounds wonderful. We'd be honored to come and lead the way to the church. Sometimes it's hard to attract people to the later service. We do an early one at five, but each year attendance dwindles at the late service. This might give us a boost."

She left him with some flyers he promised to post and hand out to the congregation. "Hope to see you in church Sunday," he said.

"I'll be working, unfortunately, but I'll be here on Christmas Eve." She thanked him and made her way back to the school, surveying the sidewalk. "As long as we don't have ice, the walk should be easy," she muttered to herself, hopping into her Jeep.

She stopped by the bakery and gave Grant a stack of flyers. He offered her some coffee. With a grateful smile, she took the cup and held it. "I'm still freezing. I can't seem to warm up no matter how many layers I wear."

He guided her to a table in the corner near the end of the counter. "It's all those years in California. They've made you soft. You have to toughen up, my friend."

She chuckled and took a sip of the warm brew. "So, I need to order some treats for the gala and need some recommendations." She went through her menu ideas. "I'm hoping if I use everyone local for the gala, they'll be more amenable to donating something for the auction." She winked several times.

"Got ya," he said. "You can count on me for a donation. How about I contribute a monthly treat box?"

"Perfect." She made a note in her folder. She ran through her list of local restaurants and made sure she had the right contact name for each one. There was only one florist. The same family owned the local nursery, so that was easy. They were great friends of Dottie's. Grant offered to have Dottie contact Bella at the flower shop.

"What about musicians? I wanted to have some instrumental Christmas music and a few performances from local choirs. If that's not doable, we can use a streaming service."

"Your best bet is Jerry Swenson at the high school. He runs the music program and they put on a Christmas concert. He could probably help you figure it out."

She added his name to the list as Grant continued. "He's in here every morning on his way to school. I'll make you his favorite coffee. You can bribe him with it." He left her to her notebook.

She caught up on her work email while she waited for the coffee. Grant returned with a large cup. "We can go up to the torchlight parade early tomorrow, take some flyers, and talk to Joe, who owns the resort. I've got an order for him for tomorrow. You can tag along."

"That would be great. I've got to get some fudge done, but I can knock off early." They made arrangements for Grant to pick her up at the house.

She drove across town to the high school, checked in at the office, and followed the directions to the music department. She found Mr. Swenson behind his desk. She held out the cup of coffee and introduced herself.

He smiled and took the cup. "Ah, Grant knows my weakness." He listened as she explained her music needs for the gala.

His eyes twinkled with excitement. "What a wonderful idea. I was hoping we could save the center somehow. I'm sure we can get some band members and choir students together for such an important event. It's Christmas break, of course, so we won't have our full ensemble, but we'll be there."

She explained the details, and he promised to set up a rehearsal for the group before school let out for the break. They exchanged numbers, and she left him with several flyers.

Sugar's stomach grumbled as she got into her Jeep. She was past hungry. The Corner Café was on her list and would have to do for lunch. Festive snowmen painted on the glass door welcomed her. A delicious savory aroma drifted through the air. She took a seat at the counter, and a cheerful woman greeted her.

"You must be Peggy's daughter," said the woman, handing Sugar a menu. "I'm Josie, the owner."

"Great to meet you. How did you know who I was?"

"Small town." She held the coffee pot up and raised her brows. "Not to mention you've got that sunny California girl look going on. Not too many people in Silver Falls look like they just came from the beach."

Sugar smiled and waved off the coffee. "I'll take water, please."

"The guys from the city were in for coffee this morning and said you've got a plan to save the arts center. That's terrific."

"That's why I'm here. Well, I'm hungry, so I'm also here for lunch. What's your soup?"

"I've got chicken vegetable and clam chowder today."

Sugar ordered the chicken vegetable and took her folder out of her tote bag. "I'd also like to order some food for the event on Christmas Eve. I'm doing appetizer stations and need a variety."

Josie brought her a steaming bowl of soup and a thick piece of bread with butter. She took off her apron, revealing a red sweater covered with white snowflakes, and sat next to Sugar. The woman took out an order pad and her pen.

The two discussed options, and Josie suggested several customer favorites. They decided on four different items. Josie did some calculations on her order pad and circled a price. "How's that sound?" she asked Sugar.

"Terrific. We'll have someone there to let you in to set up in the afternoon." Sugar took her last spoonful of soup from the bowl. "This was delicious."

"All homemade and one of my favorites. I'll put some in a takeaway container for you to take home." Josie noticed the bread remained untouched. "You didn't like the bread?"

"Oh, I'm sure it's delicious. I just try to eat gluten-free." She watched Josie ladle soup into a large cup. "I'll leave these flyers with you, and I was hoping you might be willing to donate something to the silent auction we'll be having at the gala."

"Of course. Put me down for a breakfast for four and a dinner for two." Sugar thanked her and explained how the donation campaign was designed to work, giving Josie a copy of the instructions she had written for business owners. "Looks great. I'll do my best to get some donations for you. If your numbers change, let me know, and we'll make more appetizers for you."

Sugar tried to pay for the extra soup, but Josie wouldn't have it. "Thanks for helping us save the center. You be sure and come back."

Sugar waved goodbye and set out for the Sugar Shop to get a head start on tomorrow's fudge making.

9

Hope supervised the volunteers at the arts center on Saturday, which left Sugar on her own. Hope sent her periodic texts with updates, and by three o'clock, the volunteers had succeeded in hanging all the art Sugar had selected and cleaning all the workshops and classrooms.

In the midst of her last batch of fudge, she heard a knock on the door. Grant lifted a gloved hand in greeting.

"Are you busy?" He asked as he stepped through the door.

"Making fudge, what else?" she rolled her eyes.

"I've got the cookies loaded in my truck, since we might run into snow. Everyone else is going to meet us up there later tonight."

"I need to get this batch in the cooler to chill, and then we can go." She finished the job at hand, hung up her apron, slipped into her coat, and made sure she had her hat, scarf, and gloves.

On the drive up the mountain, Grant told her he made a trip to the Tipsy Moose and Danny liked the trivia idea. "He'll do Thursday and Friday nights for the next two weeks."

"That's great. You gave him the instruction sheet for the donations?"

Grant nodded. "Yes, he's got it under control. He said he'll donate a few bottles of booze for the silent auction as well."

"Thanks for doing that. Your mom called me this morning and said Bella will let us use some of her trees and plants as decorations for free since she's doing all the centerpieces and flowers for us. She's donating a monthly vase of flowers as a prize."

"Sounds like it's all coming together."

"I checked on the online donation app I'm using. We've already gotten quite a few, so it's working." She stared out the window at the majestic trees draped in snow. "I haven't been up here since I was in high school. It's beautiful."

"Living here, I sometimes forget how lucky we are to have all this at our fingertips." He guided the truck around the curves of the road leading up to the turnoff for the ski resort.

He found a spot near the back entrance so he could unload the boxes with ease. Sugar hopped out and helped him cart in the delivery. Grant introduced her to Joe. "Joe's grandpa, Harvey, ran the resort when we were growing up, and now it's Joe's."

Sugar nodded. "I remember Harvey. Great to meet you."

"I know your mom well. Sorry to hear she's laid up. It's got to be tough with it being her busiest time of year," said Joe.

"Sugar's been doing a great job of keeping Peggy's place running, and she's taken over the handling of the fundraiser for the arts center," said Grant. "We brought you some flyers, and she can tell you all about it."

Sugar explained how businesses could help by asking customers to donate at the time of their purchase and showed him how to use the online donation function. She mentioned the silent auction. "We've got a huge sponsor in the Strumm Company. They are one of the major sponsors of the gala and are also doing an online promo for us."

"That's terrific. We carry their boards and skis at the shop. We can highlight them with a cool display." Joe took the flyers from her. "I'm happy to donate two season passes to the auction."

"That's terrific, thank you. I hope you'll be able to attend the gala."

"We wouldn't miss it," he said with a smile. "Sounds like fun." One of his staff members motioned for him. "I better run; we need to finish the set up for the parade."

"We're going to stick around for it. Thanks much, Joe." Grant shook his hand as the busy man hurried to help the staffer.

"We can grab a good table outside and save spots for everyone."

Sugar grimaced. "It's so cold."

"They've got heaters set up throughout the seating area. We'll make sure you're near one of them." He led her around the side of the lodge to the tables and chairs. He pointed at one with a prime view of the mountain. "This one with a built-in fire in the middle is perfect. Plus, it's right next to the heater."

He pulled out a chair for her. "How about something hot to drink? Cocoa, hot toddy, coffee?"

"Coffee sounds good, thanks."

While he was in the café, Sugar watched skiers and boarders get in their last runs of the day. The view up the mountain was spectacular, with beautiful white snow peppered with soaring pines. As the light of day began to dwindle, the ski patrol closed the runs and herded everyone toward the lodge. With the warmth from the heater and the fire at the table, the constant chill Sugar had was disappearing.

Grant returned with two cups and a plate of treats. "We'll save these for when Jake gets here. Drew and I brought him last year. Hope was sick with a horrible cold, and Mom was laid up with her ankle. He'd never seen a torchlight parade and was so excited."

"I remember coming to it once, with my dad. I was probably ten or eleven. We had a great time."

"They've upped their game since then. It's always a favorite festival event." He pointed to the parking area. "As you can see from the stream of people arriving now."

As the sky darkened, more and more festival goers crowded into the area. Dottie, Hope, Drew, and Jake were among them. Grant moved and sat next to Sugar to make room for the new arrivals.

Elves with lights wrapped around them bounced from table to table, handing out candy canes and chocolates to the children. Jake selected a cookie from the tray on their table and munched on it while they awaited the parade.

Soon the crowd started pointing at the top of the mountain where dots of orange glowed against the snow-covered hill. The flashes of red and orange increased and began to wind down the slope. Hope gawked and pointed at the brilliant line of lights making their way to the lodge.

Jake kept shouting at his mom to look where he gestured. Sugar's eyes went wide as she stared at the radiant light show. Grant leaned close to her ear. "I told you they had upgraded the parade since you were here."

"It's incredible, and there are so many skiers."

The crowd clapped and screeched as the brilliant orange light snaked closer. As soon as the last skier reached the bottom, the sky lit up with bursts of fireworks. A huge volley of explosions illuminated the sky, making it seem like

The Magic of the Season

daylight. Beautiful multi-colored starbursts, huge red chrysanthemums, and glittering trails of gold showered over them.

Sugar's mouth gaped open, and she leaned over to Grant. "Wow, that's new and amazing."

"See what you've been missing," said Grant, pointing at another shimmer of lights high in the sky, announced by the sizzle and hiss of dozens of launches.

Sugar joined in with Hope and Jake shouting out the shapes they saw in the colorful lights. Willows, flowers, rain, waves, and waterfalls topped off their list of images in the night sky.

After the show ended, the elves returned to each table and gave everyone sticks and marshmallows. Despite having roasted his first sweet confection only last year, Jake seized the opportunity to instruct Hope and Sugar in the finer points of the art. With their sticks loaded, they set them in the flames, turning them with precision.

Each of them, including Sugar, slid off the gooey warm morsel, and ate it. Grant pointed at Sugar. "I can't believe you ate it. Pure sugar, you know."

She smirked. "Chalk it up to peer pressure. Jake worked so hard to make sure we all knew how to roast them; I didn't want to disappoint him."

The tourists and townsfolk began to disperse. "I have a reservation for all of us at Silver Creek Pizza. Go ahead and order if you get there first," said Sugar.

Jake's eyes twinkled with excitement. "Pizza," he yelled. "This is the best day ever." Hope and Drew guided him to their SUV with Dottie trailing them.

"You know the way to Jake's heart. He loves pizza," said Grant, as they walked to the parking lot.

"I was hoping it would be a hit with everyone."

Grant steered his truck into the traffic and onto the main

road. "Drew practically lived on pizza the last few years. He worked late constantly, and if he didn't come to Mom's for dinner, he'd pick up a pizza. He's not much of a cook."

Sugar shook her head. "I have no room to talk. I'm a lousy cook and tend to grab something at the market or stop for takeout. I can't remember the last time I prepared a real meal."

"Mom and I are the cooks in the family. I enjoy it and have learned most of what I know from her." He pointed at a house decked out in tons of lights and moving decorations in the yard. "There are some great houses up here. They really get in the spirit."

In between looking at lights and Christmas villages, they talked about the fundraiser, the upcoming cookie exchange, and the ski resort. "The tiny resort I remember from my childhood has blossomed into quite the booming business," said Sugar.

"You ought to squeeze in some time for some skiing while you're here."

She laughed. "Oh, I haven't skied in years. I'm afraid I'd be joining my mom at the rehab center."

"How about snow shoeing? It's good exercise and safe. We could come up tomorrow. It's about the only day I'll have available for the next week. I'll be working nonstop starting Monday. What do you say?"

She wrinkled her nose and frowned. "It would be fun to check out the view from the mountain. But I've got so many orders to finish."

"How about I come back tonight after pizza and help with more batches? That will give you a little cushion. We can spend a few hours on the mountain, and you'll have the rest of the day to work."

She pondered as she stared at a house with dozens of blow up decorations and a miniature Ferris wheel in the yard. "I'll probably freeze to death, but okay. I'll go. It sounds fun, and who knows when I'll be back here again?"

Grant smiled and turned onto Main Street. "Great, it'll be fun." He drove past the tree towering above the buildings, twinkling with thousands of lights.

"There really isn't any place like Silver Falls at Christmas," said Sugar, as he turned on a side street and parked in front of the pizza place.

Sugar hadn't completely thawed from her excursion the night before. She woke early and started a load of towels and aprons in the washing machine before hurrying back to bed to warm her feet. After her shower, she turned her new space heater on full blast and caught up on her emails while she snuggled under her blankets.

With Grant's help, she'd made more than enough fudge to compensate for a few hours off today. They were hitting the Corner Café for breakfast before they made the trek up to the lodge. He was picking her up in less than thirty minutes.

She closed her laptop, plugged it into her new power strip, next to her tablet, and commenced layering on clothes. She heard a knock at the door as she was putting on her warmest socks.

She hurried downstairs and tossed the laundry in the dryer while Grant waited. She grabbed her coat and winter gear and followed him to his truck. She opted for an egg white omelet, while Grant devoured a platter of blueberry pancakes, eggs, bacon, and fried potatoes.

Josie set them up with coffees to go, and they headed out for the resort. The day was cold but sunny, with a pristine blue sky framing the snowy mountain. Grant turned off on a side road. "Thought we'd make a quick trip to the falls. Might as well check up on the town's namesake while we're out here."

He meandered down a narrow road and parked on a dirt turnout. He led the way up an inclined trail covered in snow. Sugar trudged behind him. He turned and said, "It'll be worth it, trust me."

"I wouldn't have to worry about a gym membership if I climbed this each morning. I can already feel it." She grunted as she reached the first turn of the trail.

"It's not much further." Grant waited for her to catch up to him. He plodded through the snow, which got thicker the higher they climbed. He stopped at a metal sign indicating their destination. "Hear that?" he asked.

She reached for his hand on the last step and strained to listen. The soft sound of a trickle of water beckoned them. They walked down a short path to the falls where a delicate stream of icy cold water seeped between cascades of solid ice. Waterfalls that surged forth in the spring and summer months had been frozen in place, creating a breathtaking winterscape framed by noble evergreens standing guard along the crest line. Frosty white water turned to ice sat motionless, as if time had stopped, as it curved and bowed over the huge rocks on its cascade to the river below.

"This was worth the hike." Sugar positioned her phone and began clicking to capture the rare beauty of winter at Silver Falls.

After spending a few more minutes admiring the view, they traveled down the trail and back to Grant's truck. He held the door and helped her tap her boots to dislodge the snow. "You should see it in the warmer months. It's roaring when the runoff is in full gear. You can hear it from down here in the parking lot."

"Another place I haven't visited for decades. Sounds like I need to make a trip back this summer."

The Magic of the Season

Grant steered them back to the main road and onward to the resort. Joe greeted them in the ski shop and helped Sugar find the proper snowshoes, telling them the best spots to visit.

Grant gave her a quick lesson in how to position her feet and raise her knees to make sure she didn't get tangled up in the two feet long shoes. They rode the gondola to the top of the mountain. The snow sparkled in the sun, like glitter sprinkled over the ground.

Once they reached the station, they took to the trail. It was slow going at first, until Sugar got the hang of the snowshoes. Grant led the way to a point that offered a panoramic view of the valley below them. Nestled in the heart of it was his beloved town of Silver Falls.

"Wow, what an awesome photo. I've got to take one." Sugar fumbled in her pocket for her phone and took several shots.

Grant took another of her against the backdrop of the stunning winter vista. She held her phone in front of her and motioned to Grant. "Come join me, and I'll take one of both of us."

He scrunched close to her, their heads touching, as she pressed the button multiple times. "The gang at work will never believe I was in the snow."

"Are you getting cold?" he asked.

She nodded. "Warmer when we're moving. It's more exercise than I thought."

"Let's go over there," he pointed to the path that led into the trees. They were the only ones on the trail. Grant stopped amid a cluster of soaring trees. The tops of the pine and cedar trees looked as if they reached the sky.

The two stood, mesmerized by the majestic forest surrounding them. The occasional soft thud of snow falling from a branch was the only sound. The snow before them was pristine, glittering in spots where the sun broke through the canopy of lofty boughs.

"Gorgeous," whispered Sugar.

"Peace," said Grant. "Standing here, I always feel at peace. The wonders of nature do that for me."

Sugar moved her sunglasses and swiped her glove under her eye. "Sorry, it's just so beautiful. I've missed this." She took out her phone and captured a few more photos.

A Christmas tune from Grant's cell phone interrupted the silence. "Hey, Mom, what's up?"

Sugar continued on the trail a few feet ahead while Grant spoke into the phone.

"Okay, I understand. We'll head back now." He put it back in his pocket and caught up with Sugar.

"There's been an incident at your mom's house. We need to get back to town," he said.

She gasped. "Oh, no. What happened?"

"It was a small electrical fire of some sort. The fire department is there now, and they're checking things."

Sugar quickened her steps. "I should have never left. I should have been there."

"Take it easy. Drew went over to the house. We'll get it figured out when we get there. You don't need to get in a big hurry and fall down," Grant said, slowing his pace.

"How much damage? Did she say?"

"They're evaluating it now. They should know everything by the time we get there."

10

Grant guided the truck down the winding road, doing his best to calm Sugar's fears and assuage her tears. "Every problem has a solution. We'll help you figure it out."

"I've got so much work to do over the next two weeks. I can't handle one more complication. I felt like I was home free after figuring out the fundraising nightmare."

Grant made the turn for Peggy's house and saw two fire department vehicles on the sidewalk. Sugar was out of the truck before he stopped, running to the front door.

Drew was on the porch and directed Sugar to the backyard. "Chief Adams, this is Peggy's daughter," he said, introducing the man wearing the white helmet.

The sharp odor of burning wires greeted them. She nodded her head as she stared at the scorched area around the electrical box. "Good news is, no real damage beyond what you see here. We broke your back door getting inside, but it can be easily repaired. It looks like a case of overloading the circuits." Chief Adams patted the side of the house with his gloved hand. "This old house isn't equipped to handle the load of modern homes."

Sugar's face whitened. "I left the heater on this morning."

The chief gave her a grim nod. "Yes, ma'am. That was a contributing factor. You had several items plugged into a power strip, plus the space heater. The load was too much, and it caused an electrical fire."

"So, it's only the outlet upstairs in my room that's out of commission?"

"Afraid not. That outlet is blackened, but the major damage is in your box. I've tagged it, so until you get an electrician in here to repair it, you're without power."

"Mom tried to tell me," she muttered. "I was too busy to listen and thought she was being overly cautious." Tears fell onto her cheeks. "How could I have been so stupid?"

Grant put an arm around her shoulders. "This is fixable." He looked at his brother. "Can you give George a call and ask him to get on this right away?"

"Sure thing." Drew took out his cell and drifted away from the others.

Grant explained George was an electrician and owned his own business. Plus, he was a customer at the bakery, and Drew took care of his dogs. "Let's get all your perishables out of the cooler and stash them at the bakery for now. Grab whatever you need, and you can stay at my place for as long as you need to."

The firemen cleared out of the yard and left Grant and Drew to help Sugar. Grant backed his truck into the driveway and started carting out the boxes of candy, butter, and other supplies from the walk-in cooler and freezer. Sugar got to work on boxing up what was in the kitchen refrigerator and freezer.

She left Drew and Grant to load everything and hurried upstairs to pack a bag. Fresh tears erupted when she saw the blackened outlet in her bedroom and smelled the stench of burnt wiring. She put her laptop and tablet in a bag and toted the space heater downstairs.

She helped them finish loading all her supplies and hopped into Grant's truck. She was quiet on the way to the bakery. He rearranged his supplies and made room for her items on the shelves. "Let's get what we can delivered tomorrow, and that will make room for more. You can use the kitchen here, but it will have to be at night. I'm slammed this week because of the cookie exchange."

"I'm sorry. I know this is a pain for you. I'm hoping George can have me back in business soon." She shook her head in disgust. "I'm also hoping not to tell Mom."

Grant chuckled. "I wouldn't count on keeping it a secret. Your mom has way too many friends here, and news like this will spread like wildfire." He stammered and blew out a breath. "I can't believe I said that. Sorry, horrible choice of words."

As she was tagging the unlabeled boxes of fudge for delivery, she broke into a hysterical laugh. Uncontrollable giggles and snorts burst from her mouth. "Sorry," she squeaked out.

He took the delivery tickets from her and guided Sugar to a chair. She was shaking and still laughing, tears streaming down her face. He brewed her a cup of tea and made her take sips from it.

"I think it's a stress response." He held the mug, not trusting her to keep it steady. "You need to take some deep breaths and try to calm down."

She gave a tiny nod and took another sip before inhaling a long breath. She took several slow breaths, and the shaking subsided. "I'm feeling better, thanks."

"Good, let's head over to Mom's. Dinner's at her house tonight. Drew and Hope will be there, and we'll get a plan together for the week."

Sugar finished her tea and helped Grant with the

remaining delivery tickets. They stopped by Grant's house to retrieve Ginger and Luna and drop off Sugar's bags. A festive Christmas tree lit up the open living area. He gave her a quick tour and showed her the guest room and all the extra supplies for the bathroom.

She held up her computer bag. "I'm afraid to try my laptop and tablet. They're probably fried."

"Don't plug them in. Just turn them on and see what happens." She opened the cover and shut her eyes as she pushed the button on the laptop. Both dogs took great interest in their guest and crowded in next to her.

Her shoulders slumped. "No luck, nothing." She did the same with the tablet. It flickered to life then fizzled. "Looks like I'll be investing in some new devices."

Grant frowned. "Are your files saved somewhere?"

She nodded. "Yes, thank goodness. I have everything automatically backed up at my office or with a cloud service. At least I didn't lose all my work." I'll order new ones, and they'll be here in a couple of days.

Grant loaded the dogs, and they headed to Dottie's. When they opened the door, the other three dogs and the rich aroma of something cooking in the kitchen welcomed them.

Drew and Hope were in the kitchen with Dottie. "Oh, Sugar, how are you, dear?" asked Dottie, coming around the island to embrace her.

"I'm okay. Embarrassed and irritated with myself, but okay." Sugar shrugged her shoulders. "As if I didn't have enough going on, right?"

"I talked to George, and he said he'll get someone over to the house first thing tomorrow. He said he's been telling Peggy she needed to address the old wiring and panel, but she's been limping along with it." Drew added, "He said it was only a matter of time before it failed like it did today."

"I've got to call Mom. I should do that before someone

else calls and tells her," said Sugar, digging her phone from her pocket.

"There's a nice quiet niche under the staircase. We only have two couples here tonight, and they're out. So nobody will bother you there." Dottie put her arm through Sugar's and led her to the staircase.

When she returned, Hope was putting together a salad, while Drew and Grant promised Jake a quick game of football before dinner. "I was going to offer Sugar a room here, but starting Thursday, I'm totally booked," said Dottie.

Grant helped himself to a cookie from the tray on the counter. "She moved some stuff into my guest room. I told her she could stay there as long as she needed. I figured you'd be booked, and I'm not sure how long it will take George to fix the wiring."

Dottie's brows arched, and she gave Hope a sly smile. "That was nice of you. I'm sure she's stressed and worried about the candy orders. I was thinking since my kitchen is inspected and approved like Peggy's, Sugar could use it to do her candy."

Grant nodded. "We moved all her supplies to the bakery, but that's a good idea. She'd be stuck doing it late at night because of my work schedule this week. This way, you two could help her." He looked at Hope and back at his mother.

"We'd be glad to help her. We'll see what she says after she's talked to Peggy. Poor girl. She's been doing such a good job." Dottie lifted the lid on one of the pots on the cooktop.

"Let's go get in that game while the sun is shining," said Drew. Jake didn't need any prodding and jumped from his chair. The two brothers followed him and the clamor of dogs outside.

Hope brewed tea while Dottie put a cake in the oven. Sugar came around the corner, her face blotchy. "How'd it go?" asked Dottie.

"She was more than upset at first. At the end of our conversation, she admitted she should have addressed the problem years ago. She's worried about me and how I'm going to get all the orders done without her kitchen."

"We were all talking about that very subject. I'd like to offer you my kitchen. It's available as soon as we're done with breakfast. Grant's bakery would be ideal, but with all the extra work this week, that would mean you'd be working in the dead of night." Dottie waved her hand along the expanse of the island. "It's got plenty of room, and it's certified and inspected, like your mom's. I don't have a spacious walk-in cooler and freezer like the bakery, so you'd have to go back and forth, but you could work during the daylight hours."

Sugar's lips curved into a tiny smile. "That would be wonderful. I can't thank you enough, Dottie. Not that I wasn't appreciative of Grant's offer, but I was dreading working nights."

Hope smiled and nodded as she slid a cup of tea to Sugar. "As soon as we finish our chores here, we'll both help you this week. It'll go faster with the three of us."

Tears filled Sugar's eyes. "I don't know what I would have done without all of you. I've missed having…all of this. People that I can count on to help." She drummed her fingers on the cool granite countertop. "I mean, I have friends; it's just different. They're more work related."

Hope put her hand over Sugar's. "I know exactly what you mean. The people in this house," she glanced at Dottie, "and in this town are like a family. They're willing to help friends or strangers. When you think all is lost, they offer you hope."

Fighting back tears, Sugar clasped her other hand over Hope's and squeezed it tight.

The back door opened with the commotion of five dogs

The Magic of the Season

and three humans charging into the house. After hanging up their coats and taking off their boots and winter gear, the men and Jake hurried through the kitchen to warm themselves in front of the fire.

"You boys get cleaned up. Dinner's ready," shouted Dottie.

Over homemade soup, salad, and bread, Dottie explained their latest idea for candy making activities. Grant nodded his agreement. "That's a great idea, Mom. Any other week and we could probably swing it at the bakery, but this is the worst timing."

Sugar grinned at Grant. "I was thinking I could do your deliveries in the morning as well as deliver the candy orders we have boxed to get them out of the way. Then I'll pick up the supplies we need and come back here and get started on the kitchen work. I'd offer to help in the bakery, but I'm pretty useless when it comes to actual cooking."

His brow wrinkled. "Delivering would be terrific. We'll see how well you remember the town. Might want to take a map with you."

"I can use my phone for directions." She poked a playful elbow at his ribs.

As they finished the meal, Sugar filled the brothers in on her conversation with her mother. Grant looked at his brother and back at Sugar. "Drew and I were talking and think it's best if you let George do whatever is necessary to fix it once and for all. You can work here and at the bakery and get your orders done. Don't be in a hurry to go back until it's fixed." Grant began gathering the dishes from the table.

"Right," said Drew. "Then Peggy won't have to worry about it in the future."

Sugar nodded. "I basically told her the same thing on the phone earlier. She wanted to know if George could repair the one outlet, and I vetoed the idea. The house needs to be safe. We don't need any more problems."

"How's she doing with her therapy?" asked Dottie. "I need to find another day to go visit."

"She said she's making good progress and gaining some strength. She told her therapist she's leaving by Christmas Eve."

Dottie chuckled. "That sounds like Peggy. She's always been determined." Dottie stood and made her way to the counter. "I've got a chocolate cake for dessert."

"I've gotta run, Mom. I've got an early start," said Grant, giving her a kiss on the cheek. "Thanks for dinner and all the help."

"I'll have cake," said Jake, picking up his fork and licking it clean.

"None for me, thanks." Sugar enveloped Dottie in a long hug. "I can't thank you enough for your kindness. You'll never know what it means to me."

"It's nothing, dear. You're like part of my family, and I'd do anything to help you. We'll see you tomorrow." Dottie patted Sugar on the back.

Grant drove to Peggy's so Sugar could pick up her Jeep. He got the dogs settled for the evening and gave Sugar a spare key so she could come and go as she needed. "I'm going to hit the hay. I'll catch up with you in the morning at the bakery."

Sugar stayed up late and using Grant's computer, ordered a replacement laptop and tablet. She submitted her supply order for the candy shop and checked her work emails. The fundraiser was still bringing in donations, and the calendars were due to arrive tomorrow. After she created some posts for social media to create buzz about the gala, she turned off the light and went to the guest room.

Once settled under the blankets, she let out a heavy sigh.

The Magic of the Season

It had been a long day. The peace she had experienced at the falls and while snowshoeing had been shattered with the frightening news of the fire. She had been running on adrenaline since that moment.

The crushing guilt she had felt from the moment she heard the news eased after talking to her mom. The Fishers had come to her rescue. She had missed so much by staying away from Silver Falls. Instead of the memories she feared, she had discovered what she'd lost. Friends. Family. People who cared.

She was almost asleep when she bolted up off her pillow. "I forgot my smoothie blender." She grinned, thinking of the ribbing Grant would subject her to if she mentioned it.

Sugar didn't budge when Grant left the house early Monday morning. The soft light of dawn woke her after six. She wandered into the kitchen, giving the dogs a few ear scratches while she poured herself a cup of the coffee Grant had brewed.

She glanced around the space and saw her power blender on the island and a note beside it. *Picked this up at your mom's this morning when I realized you didn't bring it with you. I put your veggies and gross milk in the fridge. Enjoy your green goop —Grant.*

She brought her hand to her mouth and laughed as she plugged in the blender and collected the makings for a smoothie. It had been a long time since someone, especially a man, did something so thoughtful for her.

11

The morning deliveries, with plenty of visiting and well-wishing from her customers and Grant's, made Sugar run later than she had intended. While she was dispensing pastries and candy, the local delivery driver called her and met her at the arts center to drop off the boxes of calendars. She loaded several of the boxes into the van and continued on her route. She left calendars at each of her business stops, taking a whole box to Mr. London at City Hall. When she returned, she displayed a few calendars throughout the bakery and left a stack at the register.

She loaded up the supplies for the day's candy making and made it to Dottie's a little before noon. George called as she was pulling into the driveway and gave her a ballpark figure for replacing the wiring and upgrading the panel.

She shuddered but gave her approval. He promised to keep her updated on the progress but told her it would be at least two weeks. He was running a portable generator at the house to make sure the pipes didn't freeze.

It wasn't the best news, but it wasn't much of a surprise.

Her mom had ignored the underlying problem and hobbled along with the faulty system for far too long. Sugar had more than enough in her savings to cover the cost and didn't want to leave her mom with a problem.

Hope helped her carry in the supplies, and she and Dottie jumped in to get started on the first batches. They worked and visited all afternoon, listening to Christmas music while they made Peggy's famous fudge recipes.

Plans for the holiday dominated their conversation, as did the arrival of Hope's daughter, Tina. She was spending most of her break from college with Hope. "She's used to living in Chicago with lots of excitement and things to do. I'm not sure how we'll keep her busy in Silver Falls." Hope's hesitant tone did little to hide her misgivings.

Sugar slid a pan of fudge into the freezer. "Grant and I had a great time going up to the ski resort. We stopped at Silver Falls and, although it's frozen, it's quite gorgeous. Maybe Tina would like to ski or snowshoe?"

Hope shrugged. "That sounds fun. Jake would love that."

"She could help with the gala. I'll need all the help we can muster," said Sugar.

Hope's brows arched with interest. "That's a great idea. She'd be good at that, and it would keep her occupied."

When Jake finished school, the bus dropped him at Dottie's. He sat at the table and worked on his homework, content to be the candy tester. Hope was careful to give him only tiny bites of each flavor.

By the time Drew arrived with takeout for dinner, the women had amassed stacks of boxed fudge that filled the island. Hope put her hands on her hips as she gazed at their accomplishment. "I'm going to run all this back to the bakery."

Drew handed her one of the bags from the Chinese

restaurant. "Here, this is Grant's favorite. There's plenty in there for two."

"Thanks for thinking of me." Sugar hugged both of the women and thanked them for all their help. "I'll see you all tomorrow."

The back door to the bakery was unlocked. She found Grant in the office on the computer. She held up the bag and said, "Drew sent me with dinner."

"Sounds great. I've just got to finalize my supply order." He looked up from the screen. "Do you need to do an order?"

"Did it last night at your place after you went to bed." She made several trips to empty the van and then took a seat on the other side of Grant's desk. "Thanks for bringing me my smoothie supplies this morning. I can't believe you did that."

He smiled over the top of the screen. "I know how important your green concoctions are to you. And, I knew you had a rough day." He tapped a few more keys on the computer and said, "Done."

"Speaking of my rough day, George called." She told him the gist of the situation.

"George is a good guy. He won't inflate the price, and he'll do a good job. It's smart to get it shipshape. Peggy doesn't need any more drama." He unearthed several oyster pails and grabbed two plates.

"I hate to inconvenience you for that long," she said.

"It's not a problem. It's nice to have someone around to talk to." He offered her first choice.

Sugar opted for no rice but scooped out chicken and vegetables. Grant stacked his plate high with rice and Mongolian beef. "I haven't eaten a proper meal all day. We've been slammed."

She stood up and said, "I forgot to tell you, the calendars arrived. I put some on display here." She hurried to the counter and grabbed one of them. "It looks terrific."

The Magic of the Season

As Grant shoveled in bite after bite, he flipped through the pages. "It's great. These will be popular with everyone in town."

"I'm going to deliver more of them tomorrow. I plan to do your deliveries each morning this week. It's the least I can do to help."

"That would be a big help. It saves me sending someone or going myself."

"I've got a big order for Crystal Valley next week." She grimaced and rolled her eyes. "I'm not looking forward to that drive."

"I'll take it over. Next week will be much slower for me, so I'll have time."

"That's a huge relief. I'll treat you to a dinner of your choice, a spa day, anything you want."

He grinned and laughed. "I don't think we have a spa, but I wouldn't refuse dinner."

"I owe you all way more than dinner. I'd love to do something special for your family. To thank them. Any ideas?" She folded her plate and put it in the empty takeout bag.

"How about spending Christmas with us? You and your mom. Mom would love it."

She frowned at him. "That doesn't seem like much of a gift."

"Nobody expects a gift. We help each other. It's what we do." He finished his dinner and gathered up the garbage. "I'm going to run all this outside to the dumpster."

When he returned, Sugar had her coat on and was slipping her hands into her gloves. "I'm going to head back to the house. I need to catch up on some computer work, if that's okay? My laptop should be here Wednesday."

"Sure. I'll see you there in a few minutes. Ginger and Luna will be looking for their dinner."

Work, eat, and sleep dominated Sugar and Grant's schedules the entire week. She handled the deliveries and worked on marketing the fundraiser at all her stops, made fudge until late in the afternoon, and joined Grant at the bakery for dinner.

She made time to call her mom in the mornings and caught up on her emails and anything from the office in the evenings at Grant's. She set up her new laptop and tablet, both of which were faster and more robust than the models she had fried. The progress at her mom's house was on schedule.

The donations had increased since the calendars had been distributed. She confirmed the music, food and drinks, and all the logistics required for the gala. She had secured more donations for the silent auction during her mornings on the road making deliveries.

By Friday afternoon, Grant and his crew had all the cookies made and boxed for the cookie exchange on Saturday. Sugar had all her candy orders done and delivered the last of them on Friday, so she'd have the weekend free to help Grant.

She parked the van and came through the backdoor of the bakery with takeout from Josie at the diner. Grant was in his office. His bloodshot eyes and sagging shoulders exposed his fatigue. Sugar took in the dark circles under his eyes and the five o'clock shadow that had grown into a three-day beard. He was exhausted but had promised they would go to the Tipsy Moose for a game of trivia.

She put his foil-covered plate in front of him and took the lid off her soup. "You look wrung out. I think we should skip the Moose tonight. We can go next week."

The Magic of the Season

He dug into his dinner and bobbed his head in agreement. "That sounds good to me. Tomorrow won't be as bad as far as baking, but we'll be swamped with people all day."

"I thought I'd come down Sunday and try to get as much candy made as I can so I don't have as much to do during the week. Will that work for you?"

"Sure will. I'm closed Sunday. Everyone needs a break after this week. It's all yours." He smiled and gestured to the kitchen.

When they got home, Luna and Ginger ate their dinner and snuggled into their blankets on the couch next to Grant. He hit the remote and turned on the television. Sugar clicked the keys on her laptop.

As she finished her emails and social media posts for the fundraiser, she said, "How about a movie? I've been wanting to see that new spy one." She looked up from her screen and saw Grant was asleep, as were his two furry friends.

She closed the laptop lid, tiptoed across the room, and grabbed a quilt from the chair. She put it over Grant, who nestled further into the pillows. Turning off the television, but leaving the Christmas tree lights on, she padded down the hall to bed.

Saturday morning, Sugar woke to the smell of bacon and coffee. She wandered out to the kitchen where she found Grant at the cooktop. The dogs alerted him to a visitor, and he turned. "Morning, Sugar. How about some breakfast?"

"It smells delicious, but…I probably shouldn't," she said, reaching for a mug and pouring coffee.

"Oh, come on. When's the last time you ate breakfast instead of drinking it?"

She smiled over the rim of her mug. "Okay, you've shamed me into it. If I have a heart attack, you're to blame."

He went back to cooking and loaded two plates. Followed by two attentive dogs with their noses in the air, he carried them to the island counter. Sugar took a look at the plates with fluffy eggs topped with cheese and fresh chives, slices of bacon cooked to perfection, and fruit. He added a plate of toast and said, "I know bread never touches your lips, but you're more than welcome to a slice."

"It looks wonderful, but I'm already cheating with this," she pointed to her plate. She loaded her fork with her first bite and stopped. "Hey, why aren't you at the bakery?"

"I decided to let them handle it for a couple of hours this morning. I felt like having a nice breakfast and relaxing a bit before the chaos of the day descends."

"I can still do the deliveries," she offered as she swallowed another bite. "By the way, this is scrumptious."

"They've got it handled. There aren't many today as most customers pick up their cookies. A lot of them go to the downtown businesses, and most of them don't open early. They've got your candy deliveries handled too, so don't worry about them."

Sugar ate every morsel of breakfast and hurried to get ready for the day. Grant cleaned up the kitchen and took the dogs for a walk, and when he returned, Sugar was dressed, talking to her mother on the phone.

For most of the day, Sugar helped at the bakery handing out deliveries, ringing up sales, and collecting loads of donations for the arts center. Jake and Hope stopped by in the afternoon with Jake carrying a giant bag of cookies he had collected. He held up the huge stash and said, "Can I leave my bag here with you? Drew is meeting us, and we're going to enter the snowman building contest."

Sugar took the bag and put it in a cupboard. "I'll keep it safe."

Right before the bakery was closing, Jake came rushing through the door. "Uncle Grant has to come and see our snowman. It's ginormous."

Sugar stashed Jake's cookies in her Jeep before bundling her scarf around her neck and hurrying down the street to the park where the contest was being held. Carolers dressed in Victorian costumes circled throughout the street, entertaining visitors. Carts with complimentary cookies and cocoa were positioned on every corner. The trees that lined Main Street were wrapped in tiny white lights and gave the whole downtown a magical feel.

Sugar walked around the block and took photos from several angles capturing the essence of Christmas in Silver Falls. She made her way to the edge of the park where dozens of snow people graced the grounds.

She found the Fishers in front of a huge snowman, dressed in a warm hat and scarf, sporting branches for arms, stones for his eyes and mouth, the required carrot nose, and holding a long red leash. Attached to the leash was a snow dog they had fashioned using pine branches to imitate fluffy ears and a tail. It was a perfect creation from the town vet and the dog loving family.

"Terrific job. That is so cute." Sugar positioned her phone and took more photos. "You guys stand next to it, and I'll take your picture." Jake beamed with pride as he stood next to the snowman and smiled.

The judges circled the displays, making notes on clipboards. A few minutes later, everyone quieted as the lead judge tapped the microphone to begin announcing the winners. He built the excitement starting with third place. Jake cheered and gritted his teeth as he awaited the announcement of the winner. "This year's winner is the Fisher family, Jake, Hope, and Drew. Wonderful work on your snowman and snowdog." The man held up a trophy, and Drew and Jake ran to collect it.

As the contestants were leaving the park, it began to snow. "We're heading back to Mom's for dinner," said Drew. "You guys coming?"

Grant started to answer, but Sugar interrupted. "Not tonight. I'm treating Grant to dinner." She bent down to Jake's level. "I've got your cookies in my Jeep and will drop them by tomorrow."

Grant's eyes widened. "I guess I'm going to dinner. See you guys tomorrow at Mom's." They waved as the three of them hurried to their car.

The snowflakes were getting fatter. They walked by the gazebo, and the man with the horse-drawn carriage called out to them. "How about a ride, you two? It's the best weather for it."

"Why not?" said Grant, taking Sugar's hand and urging her toward the festive red carriage.

Sugar scooted across the velvet seat to make room for Grant. She brought the warm furry blanket up to her chin and handed him the other end. "This will be warmer than walking," he said.

Their driver looped out of the park and took them across to Main Street. He went past the bakery and the beautiful tree that stood in the middle of downtown, stopping so Sugar could take some photos along the way. All the trees and lights in the shop windows made for a picturesque image. When he got to the end, he turned and took them by City Hall, around the next block.

It was decked out in all its splendor. Snow was beginning to accumulate on the trees and bushes. The snow and lights provided another perfect photo for Sugar's collection. The

The Magic of the Season

driver guided the horse back to Main Street and the tree, stopping to let them off in front of the bakery.

Grant took out his wallet, and the man waved him away. "Merry Christmas," he said. "You can pay me in pastries."

"That's a deal, Mel. I'll see you next week." Grant helped Sugar down and waved as Mel and the horses clip-clopped down the snow-covered street.

They hurried to Sugar's Jeep. She inched through the streets and parked in front of an Italian restaurant. "Your mom and Hope said you love to eat here."

"It's a great place," he said, holding the door for her. The enticing aroma of baking bread and garlic greeted them.

The hostess welcomed them, and Sugar told her they had a reservation. She seated them at a table next to a window overlooking the back of the restaurant. Sugar took the chair closest to the roaring fire adjacent to their table.

She studied the menu in between glances outside to watch falling snow accumulate on the patio used for alfresco dining in the warmer months. The surrounding plants and bushes were decorated with colorful lights.

They ordered, and she started to pass on the risotto that came with her salmon, but Grant told the waitress to bring it, and he'd eat it. He dipped a chunk of bread in oil and savored his first bite. "This is delicious." He waved the basket of bread in front of Sugar.

She shook her head. "None for me. I already cheated at breakfast today. Salmon and veggies for me tonight."

They lingered, and Grant enjoyed a second glass of wine. By the time they headed for the house, almost six inches of snow had amassed. Grant started a fire when they got home.

"We could try a movie tonight. I'm not as tired and can sleep in tomorrow," he said, turning on the television.

She was scrolling through her phone and nodded. "Wow,"

she motioned him to look at the screen. "The posts I put up today using some of the photos I took are blowing up."

"That's good, right?" He gave her a questioning look. "I don't know much about all of that online stuff."

"Thousands of people are commenting and sharing the photos. It's great. All the more exposure for the fundraiser." She beamed with excitement.

"Check out the donations." Her grin widened, and Grant's eyebrows rose.

12

Sunday it snowed again, and Sugar worked all day at the bakery making batch after batch of fudge and caramels. Grant arrived at lunch to help. By the time they finished in the afternoon, she had boxed the entire order for Crystal Valley and made a good start on her other orders for the week.

Grant's schedule eased during the week, and Sugar was able to use his kitchen starting in the mid-afternoon. He delivered her orders to Crystal Valley after the storm had passed through the area. She worked late each night, trying to get ahead of the massive number of boxes she had to have ready for the fundraiser.

On Thursday, Grant talked Drew and Hope into joining them to form a team for trivia night at the Tipsy Moose. Sugar cut her evening of candy making short and met them at the bar.

The tables were full, and the place was bustling with tourists and locals. She stopped at the bar and told Danny how much she appreciated him helping out the arts center.

"It's been terrific for business. I had tried doing these trivia nights before, but they never gained much traction. Believe me, you did me a favor. I've never been busier."

She took her water with lemon and made her way to Grant's table. "I was getting worried. Thought you were going to stand us up," he said.

"Never," she smiled. "Are you guys ready to win?"

"I wouldn't count on it," said Drew. "I can't believe how many teams are registered."

The hostess interrupted with an announcement for the teams to ready themselves for the contest. There were five rounds of ten questions. The foursome had no problem with the first round. They got them all correct. The difficulty increased with each round.

They whispered to each other, heads close together, so other tables couldn't cheat. Drew and Grant handled all the sports questions, while Hope and Sugar excelled in art and literature. Sugar was the best at pop culture and celebrity queries. Hope was the star when it came to television and movies.

Lots of laughs and two hours later, their team, dubbed Sugar's Cookies, took home the second-place award. Hope took the ribbon home for Jake and reminded Sugar about dinner at Dottie's Saturday night after the fireworks.

Ginger and Luna were waiting at the door when Sugar and Grant arrived at the house. Sugar bent down to ruffle Ginger's ears. "I forgot to tell you, I got a call from George today. He said two of his guys are out with some horrible flu, so he's going to be delayed. I'm going to need to stay another week, I think."

Grant flipped on the television. "Not a problem. Like I said, I've enjoyed having you here. I've had fun these last couple of weeks."

"Me too," said Sugar, continuing to pet the dogs as she stared at the Christmas tree. "I spend most of my time alone, so it's been nice to be here. It's comforting. You and your family. Being here in Silver Falls. Home."

She paused as she focused on the tree. She jerked her head in the other direction and stood. "I better check my emails and get to bed. See you in the morning." With quick steps, she took off down the hallway.

Grant hollered, "Good night," and then turned to the dogs and whispered, "I think Silver Falls might be working its magic on Sugar."

The dogs thumped their tails against the floor and nudged closer. He put his face close to theirs. "She might be figuring out what she's been missing."

Friday, as Sugar was getting in the Jeep to head to the bakery, the box she had been expecting from her assistant arrived. She stashed it in the guest room and hurried downtown.

The sidewalks were full of tourists in town for the last weekend of the festival before Christmas. The bakery was bustling with people picking out snacks and ordering hot drinks.

She got to work in the kitchen and had several batches made by the time the bakery closed. Grant grabbed some gloves and started boxing the fudge that was chilled. "Did you talk to your mom this morning?"

She nodded, "Yes, and she's doing great. The doctor and therapists agree if she keeps it up, she can come home on Christmas Eve. I was going to ask Drew if he might be able to pick her up, with that being the day of the gala."

"I'm sure he'll do it. He's closed that day, so it should be fine. Mom was mentioning having Peggy stay with her so she would have some help."

"I've had so much on my mind, I haven't even thought about what she's going to do at home. She can't do stairs, which is a problem at her house." She let out a sigh. "I'm going to have to go back to work after Christmas. There's no way I can take more time off to stay with her."

"Mom's business at the guest house tends to slow way down after Christmas, so she'll have time to dote on her." He smiled. "Mom is best when she has someone to help." He finished a box and slid it to the end of the counter with the others. "Actually, we all are."

"I'll call Mom again this weekend and raise the idea. She loves Dottie but will probably worry she's a burden."

"Tell her how much my mom is looking forward to it. Make it sound like she'll be helping her and keeping her company during the slow season."

She tilted her head in admiration. "Good idea. You're sneaky."

He wiggled his brows at her. "Sneaky and tired." He finished the last box and took the stack to the walk-in cooler. "I'm beat. I'm going to stop by Mom's for dinner and head home."

She waved goodbye and started her next batch. With the bakery's equipment and pans, she was able to double her batch sizes and produce more candy each night. Her goal was to get as much done as possible before Monday, when the setup and decorating for the gala would commence.

She didn't get home until midnight and found the dogs asleep next to the Christmas tree. With quiet footsteps, she went to the kitchen for a glass of water. She saw a note on the counter. *Mom sent me home with soup for you. It's in the fridge.*

It was way too late to eat, but she smiled as she took the

note, extinguished the lights on the tree, and tiptoed to her bedroom.

Her extra work on Friday afforded Sugar the opportunity to take a break for the fireworks display and dinner with the Fishers on Saturday. She captured more incredible photos of the fireworks surrounding the Christmas tree on Main Street and posted them to social media.

Jake had spent the day ice skating at the ice rink they built at the park each year and had won a prize in the gingerbread house decorating contest. He was full of excitement at dinner, giving a blow-by-blow of his day.

After dinner, Drew took his family home, Grant offered to do the dishes, and Sugar carried a cup of tea into the living room and sat next to the fire with Dottie. "I talked to Mom today and planted the seed for her staying here with you when she comes home." She shrugged and took a sip. "She didn't say no and seemed to think it made sense."

"Wonderful, I'll call her and talk to her some more about it. It really does make the most sense." She rested her hand on Scout's head. "I know what it feels like to be helpless and dependent on others. It's not easy, especially when you're trying to run a business."

"At least she won't need to worry about that. She has been doing more business around Valentine's Day, but not near as much as this time of year. She could take a break and heal until summer when the tourist season starts. I told Grant I've got to get back to work, if I expect to still have a job."

Dottie pursed her lips and shook her head. "You'd think your boss would understand the situation and cut you some slack."

"He's been very understanding, but I can tell by the tone

of his emails and by what my assistant has said, his patience is wearing thin. If it wasn't the holiday season, I'm not sure I could get away with being gone for so long."

Dottie patted Sugar's arm. "We have loved having you here. I daresay I haven't seen Grant so happy in a long time. I think it's done him a world of good to have a friend staying at his place." She brushed a tear from under her eye. "It's not easy being alone."

Sugar curled her fingers around Dottie's hand. "Being here has been wonderful for me. I realize what I've given up by not coming home for so long."

"I sure hope you come back and visit again, Sugar. You'd make us so happy, not to mention your mom."

"You can count on it," said Sugar, moving to retrieve her coat. "I've got to get back to the bakery and do a few more batches."

After working late Saturday night and putting in twelve hours on Sunday, Sugar skipped dinner at Dottie's and went to Grant's instead. She heated up the leftover soup, started a fire, and vegged out in front of the television.

When Grant returned, he found her on the couch with both dogs sprawled across her, all three, sound asleep. He left her where she was, and the dogs elected to forgo their beds and stay with her.

She slept there until morning. The sound of Grant's truck leaving woke her, but she drifted back to sleep. Her phone alarm sounded at seven, reminding her she was meeting Annie and Ryan at the old school building in an hour.

She got ready, gulped down a smoothie, gave the dogs ear rubs and a couple of cookies, and stopped by the bakery on

The Magic of the Season

her way to the school. She picked out a box of pastries, and Grant poured coffee into a portable air pot he loaned her.

He secured the lid on the pot. "How did you sleep last night? I hated leaving you there, but you were completely out." He carried the pot to her Jeep.

"Yeah, I was exhausted. I started to watch something and didn't make it five minutes." She put the box in the back seat. "The good news is, all the orders for this week are done. I've got a good start on the fundraiser candy but will probably have to work tonight and tomorrow to finish it."

He held the driver's door while she slid into the seat. "That's a huge accomplishment. We'll get those orders delivered. See you this afternoon." He shut the door and tapped the roof of the Jeep, waving as she pulled away from the curb.

Sugar had time to turn on the lights and set the coffee and pastries on a table before Ryan and three young men arrived, followed by Annie with her notebook. "Good morning. Help yourselves," said Sugar, gesturing at the table.

Each of the men grabbed something from the box and headed out the side door where there was a ramp. They got to work unloading tables and chairs. Annie and Sugar started testing and organizing hundreds of strings of white lights that would decorate the area.

Annie picked up another stack of lights. "I came in last week and noticed all the classrooms look so nice. All neat and clean and decorated. I have our janitorial staff scheduled to come in Thursday morning and clean everything to have it ready for the gala, but the classrooms won't need much."

"That was all volunteers and students. They did a great

job of getting all the artwork hung and displayed. Everyone is excited about it."

"Your posts on social media have been fantastic. We've had more comments and interest related to the festival and Silver Falls than we've ever had. It's been great. Are you getting donations?"

Sugar beamed as she plugged in another string of lights. "It's been wonderful. More than I thought. The calendars have been popular, and we're getting donations from purchases at local businesses."

The men finished unloading and started bringing in huge ladders. Sugar showed them her sketches and explained how to use the supplies to create the setting she envisioned. She spent most of the day providing guidance to the men on the ladders as they strung lights and hung fabric. The crew worked until mid-afternoon and promised to be back in the morning.

Sugar used the office to spread out her folder and notes. She checked off her list as she called the florist, caterers, music teacher, and bartenders to confirm things for Friday. With that done, she made her way back to the bakery with a quick stop at the diner for a late lunch. She took a stool at the counter.

Josie took her order and asked, "How's your mom feeling?" She turned and filled a teapot.

"She's doing much better. She'll be here for the gala."

Josie brought her a bowl of homemade soup and a pot of tea. "Your gala is the talk of the town. It's been years since we had a community-wide event on Christmas Eve. I even ordered a new dress."

"I'm glad people are enthused about the gala. I just came from the arts center where we've been getting it ready. Wait until you see it." Sugar's eyes flickered with excitement.

"My daughter is in the choir at school, and they're practicing this week to make sure they're ready." She added more hot water to the teapot. "You've done a wonderful thing, creating something memorable for everyone."

Sugar held the warm cup to her mouth as she gazed out the window at the decorations. "It's been terrific for me. It's reminded me what's special about Silver Falls. I've missed it."

13

The days flew by, with Sugar spending her mornings at the center and her afternoons and evenings at the bakery. Hope's daughter had arrived and was eager to help. She was skilled in using social media. Sugar put her in charge of those duties, as well as picking up silent auction donations and making sure the calendars were stocked at all the local businesses.

That freed Sugar up to spend all her time at the school, where she ensured every aspect of the décor was flawless. Sugar's hair was in desperate need of attention, and she squeezed in time for a color and cut at the hair salon Hope recommended.

Her nervousness about the appointment had been unnecessary. Micki, the woman who did her hair, did a fabulous job. While the color processed, Micki had chatted with Sugar and told her how excited she was to attend the gala. The salon had been swamped with appointments all week for women that wanted their hair done for the big event.

Not only was the cut and color perfect, but the price tag, even with a generous tip, had come to less than half of what

The Magic of the Season

she paid for the same thing in Santa Monica. Everywhere she went downtown, people said hello and stopped to chat and ask about Peggy or the gala. She never felt alone in Silver Falls.

It was nothing like living in Santa Monica. The only people, outside of work, who knew her by name were the baristas at the coffee place and the staff at the juicery she went to each day. She was invisible to most everyone else.

By the time Friday arrived, the center was ready. All of Sugar's hard work was about to be put to the test. After sleeping in and playing with the dogs while she lingered over coffee and a smoothie, she drove to the center.

Heavy gray clouds hovered overhead, promising to deliver the snow predicted in the forecast. Drew was on his way to pick up Dottie in Reno and was hoping to be home by noon, to avoid the storm.

The Fishers had offered to help set up and decorate for the gala, but Sugar had refused, wanting to keep it a surprise for everyone. She had sworn the city crew to secrecy, hoping each person that walked up the red-carpeted stairs and into the main auditorium would be awestruck when they saw the transformation.

She was meeting Bella from the flower shop this morning so she could add all the fresh flowers. The clean scent of pine greeted her the moment she opened the door. Beautiful barrels and crates filled with logs, pinecones, fresh greens, and lights dominated the entry area. Sugar had a few minutes before Bella was due to arrive and surveyed the building one more time. She wandered the halls, taking in the gleaming wood floors and the festive decorations in the classrooms.

She flicked the power switch Ryan had shown her and gasped when she saw the main auditorium illuminated with thousands of white lights. She had observed it while everyone was working on it, but now in the quiet, she experienced it as the guests would. Her Magic of the Season theme had come to life.

Bella arrived, and Sugar helped her place the fresh flowers around the venue, adding two stunning arrangements to the barrels in the entry hall. She had used mostly white flowers with a few touches of holly with red berries for color. Lots of glass containers filled with cranberries and candles on the tables provided an elegant ambience in the auditorium.

Fresh boughs of greenery were decorated with twinkling lights and hung across the bottom of the stage. Paired with the gorgeous red velvet curtains, it provided the perfect touch of Christmas.

When they finished, they stood back and admired the setting. The silky white fabric draped over the entire ceiling of the auditorium made for a beautiful canopy. The soft lights sparkled. "This is beyond gorgeous," said Bella. "You have quite the eye." She smiled at Sugar. "I love what you did to blend the rustic elements with all the elegance of the space. It's perfect."

They stopped at the tree and adjusted the red velvet settee Sugar had borrowed. A couple photography students had volunteered to take photos of partygoers in front of the tree. Sugar helped Bella cart her supplies back to her van and noticed the expected snow was falling from the sky.

Bella shivered and slammed the door on the van. "I'll be back later to add the lanterns to the stairs and entry. They will be gorgeous along your red carpet."

Sugar hurried back indoors and breathed a sigh of relief, pleased with the result of her design and all the work from everyone involved. Her doubts about the ability of a small town to pull off a top-notch event, worthy of one of the grand hotels in the city, had been put to rest.

The Magic of the Season

She gazed out the window, watching the gentle snowfall. "I hope the weather doesn't deter anyone."

Her cell phone rang, and she saw it was George. "Tell me you have good news."

"It's mostly good," he said. "We finished our work and tested everything. It's all working fine."

"Okay, so what's the bad news?"

"The inspector can't get to it until Monday. I begged him for permission to run the furnace, and he acquiesced but said nobody could occupy the place until he's completed the final inspection on Monday."

"That's okay. Mom is going to stay with Dottie for the next few weeks, so it'll work out. I'm leaving Monday but will leave a check with Grant at the bakery. I don't want Mom to know the cost of this."

"Got it. No problem. I'll see you at the gala tonight. Merry Christmas, Sugar."

She wished him the same, grabbed her purse, and locked the doors.

She hurried downtown to pick up a few last-minute gifts. She had been so busy, and it had been years since she had to worry about buying gifts. The Fishers had been so kind, and she wanted to find each of them something special. It took several stops, but she completed her shopping mission, even picking up a beautiful gift-wrapped box for her mom.

As she drove to Dottie's, she noticed the snow was getting heavier and sticking. She stashed her bags of presents on the porch. Hope let her inside where the five dogs stood wagging their tails.

"Come on back in the kitchen. Dottie is working on pies for tomorrow, and we're visiting."

"I'll be right there. I need to run back to the car." Sugar dashed outside and, without making a noise, stashed her gifts under the tree. She took off her coat and boots and carried Peggy's present into the kitchen.

"I wanted to put this in my mom's room. I got her a fancy dress for the gala tonight as a welcome home gift."

"Oh, how wonderful," said Dottie. "I've got her downstairs in the Blue Room. Just down the hall." She gestured with her hand.

Sugar put the package on the bed, noticing the fresh flowers on the bedside table and the comfortable furnishings. She understood why the guest house was so busy.

When she returned, Hope was putting her cell phone on the counter. "That was Drew. They got a late start leaving the rehab center, so they're taking it slow. He said he'd call with updates."

"Those darned places take forever to discharge people. It's so irritating," said Dottie, adding the crust to the top of a pie.

"Especially in bad weather. They don't need the stress of that drive in the snow. I feel terrible," said Sugar.

"Drew is a very careful and experienced driver. Don't worry," said Dottie with a wink.

"I should get going. Call me and let me know if you hear more from Drew." Sugar gathered her coat and boots, promising to see them soon.

She made her way to the bakery and found Grant in his office. The bakery had closed at noon, and he was working on his computer. She handed him a check and asked him to get it to George on Monday.

"I wondered when you were flying out. I sort of hated to ask, hoping you'd stay until January."

Her eyes softened. "I'd like that, but my boss has been hinting in his emails that he expects me back right after Christmas. With Dottie helping Mom, it'll allow me to go and not worry about her."

"We're sure going to miss you," he said, leaning back in his chair. "Ginger and Luna have loved having you around the house."

She smiled. "I'll miss all of you. More than you can imagine. I'll be back this summer though. I want to go to the falls."

"I'll hold you to it." An awkward silence passed between them as they stared at each other.

Sugar stood and said, "I'll go ahead and load up the boxes of candy for the gala. Then I've got to get ready. I'll see you there tonight?"

"Wouldn't miss it for the world." He stood and helped carry the large boxes to her Jeep. They were filled with tiny red boxes of candy that would be placed on the tables for everyone attending the gala.

She trudged through the snow to take the boxes up the ramp rather than the stairs. When she was leaving, she saw Ryan and several men in heavy jackets shoveling the walkways and stairs.

She gave them a wave as she drove away, thankful they were so responsive. From the look of it, the snow wouldn't be letting up anytime soon. They were going to be stuck shoveling all night.

Grant wasn't home when she got there. The house was quiet with the dogs spending the day at Dottie's. Her phone chimed, and she saw a voicemail from Drew. "This blasted town and its cell service," she muttered, poking at her phone.

His message said they were stuck on the highway waiting for an accident to clear. They were fine and had plenty of fuel, blankets, and snacks and would do their best to get home in time for the gala.

She tossed the phone on the bed, stomping to the bathroom. "Why did we have to get a huge snow storm today of all days?" She droned on as she went about her preparations. She spent the next hour getting ready, finally slipping on the gown her assistant had mailed to her.

The gorgeous red dress fell to the floor, with beads and sequins in the bodice providing a hint of sparkle. She added shimmery earrings and took one last look in the mirror. After adding her silver heels to her bag, she put on her boots and donned her heavy coat.

She took the snow packed roads slow and parked on the side of the old school. She trudged up the ramp, which had been cleaned of snow, stomped on the mat inside the door, and changed into her heels.

She stashed her things in the office and went to the front door. Ryan and his crew were still stationed on the portico, keeping the area cleared of snow. They had installed portable heaters along the edge of the space to keep it warm. She opened the door and said, "I'm so sorry you guys are stuck working in this weather."

Ryan's red cheeks filled with a smile. "Ah, we're used to it. We're going to get a few heat mats and put them under your red carpet to keep the snow from accumulating. Bella came by to put out the lanterns, but we told her we'd do it when we put out the carpet."

"That's terrific, thanks. The caterers are due any minute, so I'll be around if you need me."

She went to the side door and found the first of the delivery vans pulling to a stop. Soon, all except Grant had arrived and were busy setting up their food warmers and displays.

The men arrived from the Elk's Lodge with ice and boxes

The Magic of the Season

of supplies for the bar. Mr. Swenson followed with his students and their instruments. They made for the stage and went about warming up and practicing while the caterers finished setting up their appetizers.

Josie was the last to finish her appetizers. Her sliders, meatballs, and pigs in a blanket smelled delicious. Sugar stepped up to her table and straightened one of the signs. "Your dress is stunning," said Josie. "This place is amazing. I can't believe it's our old school. You've done such a wonderful job."

"I had a ton of help. Everyone has worked so hard. It's going to be such fun."

"I'll be back in a jiffy. Need to run home and change for the big event." She hurried to the side door, and Sugar waved to her while she strained to look for Grant's van.

The red carpet had been installed, and the lanterns were glowing with candles and mini lights. Sugar retrieved her cell phone from the office to capture some photos before people arrived. She saw a message from Grant that he was running late.

Drew had also texted and reported they were inching along the highway, about twenty miles away. She checked the time and shook her head. There was no way they would get there before it started.

She turned off the harsh lighting and flipped the switch to activate the twinkle lights. Then she added the stage lighting. The students oohed and aahed as they looked out into the auditorium.

Bella arrived early and went about lighting the candles on all the tables. Soft instrumentals filled the air. Sugar checked on the front entrance and saw a few cars parking. She returned to the auditorium and leaned against one of the columns at the head of the stairs. She jumped at the tap on her shoulder. Grant stood before her, decked out in a black tuxedo with touches of red in his vest, tie, and pocket square.

"Wow, I've never seen you in anything but jeans and your bakery shirts. You look so handsome."

He took her hand. "That dress sure does beat your usual black shirts and apron. You look stunning in red." He waved his arm across the space. "I can't believe how you've transformed this old school into a beautiful winter wonderland. You're amazing."

Her cheeks flushed. "I enjoyed doing it. More than I would have guessed. It would have been more fun without the stress of making a million pounds of fudge, but I loved doing it." She looked down at the tables. "By the way, where are my desserts?"

"I have my staff bringing them. They're getting everything as we speak."

Annie interrupted their conversation. "Uh, Sugar, the mayor needs to see you right away. He's in the office."

Sugar turned to Grant with a cringe. "That doesn't sound good. I'll be right back." She hurried to follow Annie.

Grant watched her until she disappeared around the corner and then went to supervise the set-up of the cookies, cupcakes, and smores station.

Guests began arriving in droves. Women were outfitted in their finest dresses, some wearing fancy coats embellished with fur. Men wore suits and ties or sport jackets. Children, dolled up in their Sunday best, took parents by the hand to show them their classrooms and artwork.

Names and bids were already scribbled onto the clipboards at the silent auction table. The party was in full swing by the time Sugar emerged from the office.

She found her way to the punch bowl and gulped down a cup of the fizzy, sugar-laden drink. She scanned the crowd for Drew or Grant. She checked the time and saw it was well past the hour she had intended to take the stage and welcome everyone.

She hustled up the stairs and down the hallway, slipping through the stage entrance. She caught Mr. Swenson's eye and gave him a nod.

He brought their current piece to a close, and Sugar walked out on stage. She took the microphone and said, "Ladies and gentlemen." She tapped the microphone a couple of times to get their attention and said it again.

The crowd quieted down, and she looked out, still searching for a sign of Drew and her mother. "I want to welcome you to the first annual gala for the Silver Falls Arts Center. Thank you for coming and for the outpouring of support. We plan to do an event like this each year and hope we can count on your help. I'm Madison, or Sugar, as most people know me. You all know my mother, Peggy White. Her accident threw a wrench in her plans this year, but I was happy to step in and carry out her vision of this wonderful Christmas Eve celebration."

She waited for the applause to die down. "She's on her way here. In fact, I expected her to be here by now. The theme for this year's event is The Magic of the Season. It's quite fitting for this quaint town nestled in the valley of our beautiful mountains. This town, all of you, carry the magic of the season in your hearts each and every day. I've been gone for so long, I'd almost forgotten how incredible it is to live in such a lovely place full of caring people."

People talking and clapping along the side of the stage distracted her. She turned to discover what the commotion was and saw Peggy on Grant's arm, using a cane, as she walked down the hall. She was wearing the burgundy dress with the beaded jacket Sugar had bought for her.

People sitting stood up, and the entire audience erupted into applause and cheers. Sugar laughed and motioned them to the stage. "Someone knows how to make an entrance," she quipped.

Sugar met them at the edge of the stage and enveloped her mom in a long hug. "I'm so glad you're here."

Tears streamed down Peggy's face. "I've never seen it more beautiful than this. It's even lovelier than I imagined."

Sugar whispered, "Wait until you get a load of the donation total. You won't believe it."

Sugar offered the microphone to her mother. With reluctance, Peggy took it and said, "Merry Christmas, Silver Falls. Thank you for coming and a huge thank you to my daughter, Sugar, for all the work she did to save the arts center. She just told me we've exceeded our donation needs."

The crowd cheered and hooted. She handed the microphone back to Sugar, and Grant helped her from the stage.

"Please enjoy the lovely music, food, and drinks. Remember to take a look at all the artwork in the classrooms and don't forget to bid on one of our silent auction items. Merry Christmas." Sugar returned the microphone and exited the stage as the band played "We Wish You a Merry Christmas."

Grant was waiting for Sugar and offered her his arm. "You're beautiful, you know that? I've never seen you smile as much as you have tonight."

"I'm happy. Mom looks great, and she's thrilled. It makes all this worth it."

"She's loving all this." He pointed to her at the special table Sugar had set up in a balcony area, where her mom wouldn't have to use the stairs. She was surrounded by townsfolk, visiting and laughing.

Sugar took Grant's hand in hers and led him to a quiet hallway. "What would you say if I told you I wasn't going to make a trip to Silver Falls this summer after all?"

His face fell. "What? You promised."

She winked and smiled. "I'm not leaving." She watched as confusion flashed across his face.

"Mayor Douglas just offered me a job. He wants me to take over marketing and public relations for the city and assume the directorship of the arts center." She gripped his hand tighter. "I said yes."

He smiled, and his eyes sparkled. He picked her up off the floor and twirled her around several times. "This is the best Christmas gift I could have hoped for." He covered her lips with his in a long kiss.

When their lips parted, he leaned his forehead against hers. "I love you, Sugar. I tried not to. I didn't want to fall for a big-city girl and have my heart broken, but I couldn't help it."

"I love you too." She kissed him again.

They walked, arm in arm, taking a hallway that led to the old library, where it was quiet. Sugar looked up at Grant. "I had resolved myself to the idea that I'd be alone. I had my job, which took up most of my waking hours, and didn't think I'd find anyone."

"After Lisa, I thought the same thing. Who would I find in Silver Falls?" Grant smiled at her, pushing his shoulder against her. "I have to admit, when you first got here, you mostly irritated me."

She feigned shock, bringing her hand to her chest. "Throwing coffee on my silk blouse didn't do much for me either." She laughed and rested her head against his shoulder.

Grant put his arm around her. "The more time we spent together, I started to fall for you. I tried not to, but then when you had to move in, I realized I was fighting a losing battle. For the first time, I'm happy to surrender."

"I never thought I could be happy in Silver Falls. I liked the excitement of my job, the beach, life in the city, smoothies on every corner." She winked and laughed. "But this place has something no city has." She met his questioning eyes. "You," she said, smacking his shoulder. "You, your family, my mom, all the wonderful people who live here and go out of their way to help others. It's all right here."

They had made a loop and were steps away from the main hallway and the celebration. "Let's go get our photo taken in front of the tree. I want to remember this night forever," she said.

An hour before the gala was due to end, Grant sought out Sugar. He whispered in her ear, and she excused herself from the table where she had been visiting with Dottie and thanking Drew for the trouble he went through bringing Peggy home. She followed him to the entrance, and he held her coat.

"Where are we going?"

"You'll see," he said, gripping her hand in his, as he led her out the front door and down the red carpet.

At the bottom of the steps, Mel and his horse drawn carriage were waiting. Grant helped her settle into the seat and climbed in after her. They snuggled under the heavy velvet throw, and Mel snapped the reins.

The snow had stopped falling, leaving behind a soft blanket of white enveloping the entire town of Silver Falls. With the lights and tree reflecting in the unblemished snow, it looked like a Christmas card. The soft jingle of the bells on the horses was the only sound to be heard. The town was quiet. Everyone was at the gala.

Grant took her gloved hand in his. "I had planned this before your news. I intended to try to convince you to stay in Silver Falls."

"How were you going to do that?"

The Magic of the Season

He reached in his pocket and pulled out a velvet box. "By asking you to marry me."

Sugar gasped and looked at the sparkling ring nestled in the soft red satin. She looked into his eyes and said, "Yes, I'll marry you." She kissed him as they passed by the tree on Main Street.

Leaning her head against his shoulder, she said, "Let's not tell anyone until tomorrow. I haven't told Mom or the others about the mayor's offer."

"My mom and your mom are going to go crazy, you know that, right?" He put his arm around her and snuggled closer.

"As Jake would say, it'll be the best Christmas ever." They laughed as the carriage approached the edge of the park. Sugar pointed to the procession of people holding candles as they walked from the school to church for the Christmas Eve Service.

"We better hurry up, they'll wonder where we are," she said.

"I say let them wonder." Grant hollered at Mel to take another lap before returning them to the school building.

As the driver guided them past the gazebo, they heard the voices of the choir singing "Silent Night" as it made its way down the red-carpeted steps flanked by the flickering lanterns. She gripped his hand tighter and said, "It really is the most wonderful time of the year."

EPILOGUE

The Magic of the Season is the second book in the Christmas at Silver Falls Series. If you missed the first book, *A Season for Hope*, you'll want to download it. Along with these two Christmas stories, she's also written *Christmas in Snow Valley*, a heartwarming small-town story about a woman who returns home to spend Christmas with her sister for the first time in several years.

Tammy loves writing Christmas stories and teamed up with some author friends to write a connected Christmas series centered around a woman who welcomes four foster girls into her home during the holiday season, releasing in 2020.

If you've missed any of Tammy's Christmas stories, you can find them all at Amazon.

A Season for Hope: Christmas in Silver Falls Book 1
The Magic of the Season: Christmas in Silver Falls Book 2
Christmas in Snow Valley: A Hometown Christmas Novella

The connected Christmas series Tammy wrote with four

other authors is The SOUL SISTERS AT CEDAR MOUNTAIN LODGE SERIES. You can find all the books at Amazon.

Book 1: Christmas Sisters – perma-FREE prologue book
Book 2: Christmas Kisses by Judith Keim
Book 3: Christmas Wishes by Tammy L. Grace
Book 4: Christmas Hope by Violet Howe
Book 5: Christmas Dreams by Ev Bishop
Book 6: Christmas Rings by Tess Thompson

ACKNOWLEDGMENTS

I've always loved Christmas and the lights and trees are my favorite things about the season. This is a sequel to the novella I released in 2018, *A Season for Hope*, which was inspired by a chance encounter with a young woman in my hometown right before Thanksgiving. Along with my readers, I fell in love with the characters and decided to write another holiday story set in Silver Falls for 2019. I've fashioned Silver Falls after my own hometown and our wonderful Christmas celebrations.

My thanks to my editors, Connie and Jaime, for finding my mistakes and helping me polish *The Magic of the Season*. I plan to release this book only in eBook format, since it is a special novella for the holidays. It's meant to serve up warm wishes to you, regardless of the season in which you're reading it.

I hope you enjoyed this holiday story and appreciate all of the readers who have taken the time to provide a review on Amazon. These reviews are especially important in promoting future books, so if you enjoy my novels, please consider leaving a review. Follow this link to my author page and select a book to leave your review at www.amazon.com/author/tammylgrace. I also encourage you to follow me on Amazon and BookBub, where leaving a review is even easier and you'll be the first to know about new releases and deals.

Remember to visit my website at www.tammylgrace.com and join my mailing list for my exclusive group of readers. I've also got a fun Book Buddies Facebook Group. That's the best place to find me and get a chance to participate in my giveaways. Join my Facebook group at https://www.facebook.com/groups/AuthorTammyLGraceBookBuddies/ and keep in touch—I'd love to hear from you.

Wishing you the magic of the season,

Tammy

FROM THE AUTHOR

Thank you for reading THE MAGIC OF THE SEASON. If you haven't yet read the first book with these characters, A SEASON FOR HOPE, you'll want to add it to your list. If you're a new reader and enjoy women's fiction, you'll want to try my Hometown Harbor Series, filled with the complex relationships of friendship and family. Set in the picturesque San Juan Islands in Washington, you'll escape with a close-knit group of friends and their interwoven lives filled with both challenges and joys. Each book in the series focuses on a different woman and her journey of self-discovery. Be sure and download the free novella, HOMETOWN HARBOR: THE BEGINNING. It's a prequel to FINDING HOME that I know you'll enjoy.

For mystery lovers, I write a series that features a lovable private detective, Coop, and his faithful golden retriever, Gus. If you like whodunits that will keep you guessing until the end, you'll enjoy the COOPER HARRINGTON DETECTIVE NOVELS.

The first book, BEACH HAVEN, in my new GLASS BEACH COTTAGE SERIES is also loved by readers. It is a

From the Author

heartwarming story of a woman's resilience buoyed by the bonds of friendship, an unexpected gift, and the joy she finds in helping others. As with all my books, the furry four-legged characters play a prominent role.

I'd love to send you my exclusive interview with the canine companions in the Hometown Harbor Series as a thank-you for joining my exclusive group of readers. You can sign up www.tammylgrace.com and click on the banner at the top.

Below you will find links to the electronic version of all of Tammy's books available at Amazon

MORE BOOKS BY TAMMY L. GRACE

HOMETOWN HARBOR SERIES

Hometown Harbor: The Beginning FREE prequel

Finding Home

Home Blooms

A Promise of Home

Pieces of Home

Finally Home

Forever Home

Hometown Harbor Series Books 1-3

COOPER HARRINGTON DETECTIVE SERIES

Killer Music

Deadly Connection

Dead Wrong

Cooper Harrington Detective Novels Books 1-3

CHRISTMAS STORIES

A Season for Hope (Christmas in Silver Falls Book 1)

The Magic of the Season (Christmas in Silver Falls Book 2)

Christmas in Snow Valley

Christmas Sisters (Soul Sisters at Cedar Mountain Lodge Book 1)

Christmas Wishes (Soul Sisters at Cedar Mountain Lodge Book 3)

GLASS BEACH COTTAGE SERIES

Beach Haven

WRITING AS CASEY WILSON

A Dog's Hope

A Dog's Chance

Don't miss the **SOUL SISTERS AT CEDAR MOUNTAIN LODGE**,

a connected Christmas series centered around a woman and the four foster girls she welcomes into her home.

Christmas Sisters, Book 1, by Ev Bishop, Tammy L. Grace, Violet Howe, Judith Keim, & Tess Thompson

Christmas Kisses, Book 2, by Judith Keim

Christmas Wishes, Book 3, by Tammy L. Grace

Christmas Hope, Book 4, by Violet Howe

Christmas Dreams, Book 5, by Ev Bishop

Christmas Rings, Book 6, by Tess Thompson

If you've enjoyed Tammy's work, please consider leaving a quick review on Amazon, Goodreads, or Bookbub. They are so very helpful and essential to authors wishing to market their books. Just a quick sentence is enough! To the readers who have taken the time to leave a review, Tammy sends her heartfelt appreciation.

Tammy would love to connect with readers on social media and her website at www.tammylgrace.com. Remember to subscribe to her mailing list and you'll receive the fun interview she did with the dogs from her Hometown Harbor Series as an exclusive free gift only available to her subscribers. **Subscribe here: https://wp.me/P9umIy-e**

Connect with Tammy on Facebook and click over and follow Tammy on BookBub and Amazon by clicking the follow buttons on those pages.

ABOUT THE AUTHOR

Tammy L. Grace is a USA Today Bestselling Author of the award-winning Cooper Harrington Detective Novels, the best-selling Hometown Harbor Series, the Glass Beach Cottage Series, and several Christmas novellas. Tammy also writes under the pen name of Casey Wilson and has released *A Dog's Hope* and *A Dog's Chance*, both about the emotional connection we have with dogs. You'll find Tammy online at www.tammylgrace.com where you can join her mailing list and be part of her exclusive group of readers. Connect with Tammy on Facebook, Instagram, or Twitter.

- facebook.com/tammylgrace.books
- twitter.com/TammyLGrace
- instagram.com/authortammylgrace
- amazon.com/author/tammylgrace